Dearest
Mary Smith
Happy ready
Aunt Cashi
Uncle Rem

THE LITTLE MERMAID

AND OTHER FAIRY TALES

THE LITTLE MERMAID

AND OTHER FAIRY TALES

Hans Christian Andersen

DOVER PUBLICATIONS, INC.
Mineola, New York

EDITOR OF THIS VOLUME: JANET BAINE KOPITO

Bibliographical Note

This Dover edition, first published in 2002, is an original selection of twelve unabridged stories from *Andersen's Fairy Tales,* edited by Margherita O. Osbourne, published by The Penn Publishing Company, Philadelphia, in 1930. The story "The Little Match Girl" is from a standard edition.

Library of Congress Cataloging-in-Publication Data

Andersen, H. C. (Hans Christian), 1805–1875.
    The little mermaid and other fairy tales / Hans Christian Andersen.
        v. cm. — (Dover evergreen classics)
    Originally published: Philadelphia : Penn Pub., 1930.
    Contents: The little mermaid — The ugly duckling — The tinder box — The Emperor's new clothes — Great Claus and Little Claus — The princess on the pea — The swineherd — The red shoes — The steadfast tin soldier — Thumbelina — The little match girl — The nightingale — The Snow Queen.
    ISBN 0-486-42365-4 (pbk.)
    1. Fairy tales—Denmark. 2. Children's stories, Danish—Translations into English. [1. Fairy tales. 2. Short stories.] I. Title. II. Series.

PZ8.A542 Lit 2002b
839.8'136—dc21
[[Fic]]

                                                                        2002073995

Manufactured in the United States of America
Dover Publications, Inc., 31 East 2nd Street, Mineola, N.Y. 11501

Contents

The Little Mermaid

FAR out at sea the water is as blue as the bluest corn-flower, and as clear as the clearest crystal, but it is very deep, and if many steeples were piled on the top of one another they would not reach from the bed of the sea to the surface of the water. It is down there that the Mermen live.

The most wonderful trees and plants grow there, and such flexible stalks and leaves, that at the slightest motion of the water they move as if they were alive. All the fish, big and little, glide among the branches just as, up here, birds glide through the air. The palace of the Merman King lies in the very deepest part; its walls are of coral and the long pointed windows of clearest amber, but the roof is made of mussel shells which open and shut with the lapping of the water.

The Merman King had been for many years a widower, but his old mother kept house for him; she was a clever woman, but so proud of her noble birth that she wore twelve oysters on her tail, while the other grandees were only allowed six. Otherwise she was worthy of all praise, especially because she was so fond of the little mermaid princesses, her grandchildren. They were six beautiful children, but the youngest was the prettiest of all, her skin was as soft and delicate as a roseleaf, her eyes as blue as the deepest sea, but like all the others she had no feet, and instead of legs she had a fish's tail.

All the livelong day they used to play in the palace in the great halls, where living flowers grew out of the walls.

When the great amber windows were thrown open the fish swam in, just as the swallows fly into our rooms when we open the windows, but the fish swam right up to the little princesses, ate out of their hands, and allowed themselves to be patted.

Outside the palace was a large garden, with fiery red and deep blue trees, the fruit of which shone like gold, while the flowers glowed like fire on their ceaselessly waving stalks. The ground was of the finest sand, but it was of a blue phosphorescent tint. There was a wondrous blue light down there; you might suppose yourself high up in the air, with only the sky above and below you. In a dead calm you could just catch a glimpse of the sun like a purple flower with a stream of light radiating from its calyx.

Each little princess had her own little plot of garden, where she could dig and plant whatever she liked. One made her flower-bed in the shape of a whale, another thought it nice to have hers like a little mermaid; but the youngest made hers quite round like the sun, and she would only have flowers of a rosy hue like its beams. She was a curious child, quiet and thoughtful, and while the other sisters decked out their gardens with all kinds of extraordinary objects which they got from wrecks, she would have nothing but the rosy flowers like the sun up above, except a statue of a beautiful boy. It was hewn out of the purest white marble and had gone to the bottom from some wreck.

Nothing gave her greater pleasure than to hear about the world of human beings up above; she made her old grandmother tell her all that she knew about ships and towns, people and animals. But above all it seemed strangely beautiful to her that up on the earth the flowers were scented, and that the woods were green, and that the fish which were to be seen among the branches could sing so loudly and sweetly that it was a delight to listen to them. You see, the grandmother called little birds fish, or the mermaids would not have understood her, as they had never seen a bird.

"When you are fifteen," said the grandmother, "you will be allowed to rise up from the sea and sit on the rocks in the moonlight, and look at the big ships sailing by, and you will also see woods and towns."

One of the sisters would be fifteen in the following year, but the others,—well, they were each one year younger than the other, so that the youngest had five whole years to wait before she would be allowed to come up from the bottom, to see what things were like on earth. But each one promised the others to give a full account of all that she had seen, and found most wonderful on the first day. Their grandmother could never tell them enough, for there were so many things about which they wanted information.

None of them was so full of longings as the youngest, the very one who had the longest time to wait, and who was so quiet and dreamy. Many a night she stood by the open windows and looked up through the dark blue water which the fish were lashing with their tails and fins. She could see the moon and the stars; it is true, their light was pale but they looked much bigger through the water than they do to our eyes. When she saw a dark shadow glide between her and them, she knew that it was either a whale swimming above her, or else a ship laden with human beings. I am certain they never dreamed that a lovely little mermaid was standing down below, stretching up her white hands towards the keel.

The eldest princess had now reached her fifteenth birthday, and was to venture above the water. When she came back she had hundreds of things to tell them, but the most delightful of all, she said, was to lie in the moonlight on a sandbank in a calm sea, and to gaze at the large town close to the shore, where the lights twinkled like hundreds of stars; to listen to music and the noise and bustle of carriages and people, to see the many church towers and spires, and to hear the bells ringing; and just because she could not go on shore she longed for that most of all.

Oh! how eagerly the youngest sister listened, and when later in the evening she stood at the open window and looked up through the dark blue water, she thought of the big town with all its noise and bustle, and fancied that she could even hear the church bells ringing.

The year after, the second sister was allowed to mount up through the water and swim about wherever she liked. The sun was just going down when she reached the surface, the most beautiful sight, she thought, that she had ever seen. The whole sky had looked like gold, she said, and as for the clouds! well, their beauty was beyond description, they floated in red and violet splendor over her head, and, far faster than they went, a flock of wild swans flew like a long white veil over the water towards the setting sun; she swam towards it, but it sank and all the rosy light on the clouds and water faded away.

The year after that the third sister went up, and being much the most venturesome of them all, swam up a broad river which ran into the sea. She saw beautiful green, vineclad hills; palaces and country seats peeping through splendid woods. She heard the birds singing, and the sun was so hot that she was often obliged to dive to cool her burning face. In a tiny bay she found a troop of little children running about naked and paddling in the water; she wanted to play with them, but they were frightened and ran away. Then a little black animal came up, it was a dog, but she had never seen one before; it barked so furiously at her that she was frightened and made for the open sea. She could never forget the beautiful woods, the green hills and the lovely children who could swim in the water although they had no fishes' tails.

The fourth sister was not so brave, she stayed in the remotest part of the ocean, and, according to her account, that was the most beautiful spot. You could see for miles and miles around you, and the sky above was like a great glass dome. She had seen ships, but only far away, so that they looked like seagulls. There were grotesque dolphins turning somersaults, and gigantic whales squirting water through their nostrils like hundreds of fountains on every side.

Now the fifth sister's turn came. Her birthday fell in the winter, so that she saw sights that the others had not seen on their first trips. The sea looked quite green, and large icebergs were floating about, each one of which looked like a pearl, she said, but was much bigger than the church towers built by men. They took the most wonderful shapes, and sparkled like diamonds. She had seated herself on one of the largest, and all the passing ships sheered off in alarm when they saw her sitting there with her long hair streaming loose in the wind.

In the evening the sky became overcast with dark clouds; it thundered and lightened, and the huge icebergs, glittering in the bright lightning, were lifted high into the air by the black waves. All the ships shortened sail, and there was fear and trembling on every side, but she sat quietly on her floating iceberg watching the blue lightning flash in zigzags down on to the shining sea.

The first time any of the sisters rose above the water she was delighted by the novelties and beauties she saw; but once grown up, and at liberty to go where she liked, she became indifferent and longed for her home; in the course of a month or so they all said that after all their own home in the deep was best, it was so cozy there.

Many an evening the five sisters interlacing their arms would rise above the water together. They had lovely voices, much clearer than any mortal, and when a storm was rising, and they expected ships to be wrecked, they would sing in the most seductive strains of the wonders of the deep, bidding the seafarers have no fear of them. But the sailors could not understand the words, they thought it was the voice of the storm; nor could it be theirs to see this Elysium of the deep, for when the ship sank they were drowned, and only reached the Merman's palace in death. When the elder sisters rose up in this manner, arm-in-arm, in the evening, the youngest remained behind quite alone, looking after them as if she must weep, but mermaids have no tears and so they suffer all the more.

"Oh! if I were only fifteen!" she said, "I know how fond I shall be of the world above, and of the mortals who dwell there."

At last her fifteenth birthday came.

"Now we shall have you off our hands," said her grandmother, the old queen dowager. "Come now, let me adorn you like your other sisters!" and she put a wreath of white lilies round her hair, but every petal of the flowers was half a pearl; then the old queen had eight oysters fixed on to the princess's tail to show her high rank.

"But it hurts so!" said the little mermaid.

"You must endure the pain for the sake of the finery!" said her grandmother.

But oh! how gladly would she have shaken off all this splendor, and laid aside the heavy wreath. Her red flowers in her garden suited her much better, but she did not dare to make any alteration. "Good-by," she said, and mounted as lightly and airily as a bubble through the water.

The sun had just set when her head rose above the water, but the clouds were still lighted up with a rosy and golden splendor, and the evening star sparkled in the soft pink sky, the air was mild and fresh, and the sea as calm as a millpond. A big three-masted ship lay close by with only a single sail set, for there was not a breath of wind, and the sailors were sitting about the rigging, on the crosstrees, and at the mastheads. There was music and singing on board, and as the evening closed in, hundreds of gaily colored lanterns were lighted—they looked like the flags of all nations waving in the air. The little mermaid swam right up to the cabin windows, and every time she was lifted by the swell she could see through the transparent panes crowds of gaily dressed people. The handsomest of them all was a young prince with large dark eyes; he could not be much more than sixteen, and all these festivities were in honor of his birthday. The sailors danced on deck, and when the prince appeared among them hundreds of rockets were let off making it as light as day, and frightening the little mermaid so much that she had to dive under the water. She soon ventured up again, and it was just as if all the stars of heaven were falling in showers round about her. She had never seen such magic fires. Great suns whirled round, gorgeous fire-fish hung in the blue air, and all was reflected in the calm and glassy sea. It was so light on board the ship that every little rope could be seen, and the people still better. Oh! how handsome the prince was, how he laughed and smiled as he greeted his guests, while the music rang out in the quiet night.

It got quite late, but the little mermaid could not take her eyes off the ship and the beautiful prince. The colored lanterns were put out, no more rockets were sent up, and the cannon had ceased its thunder, but deep down in the sea there was a dull murmuring and moaning sound. Meanwhile she was rocked up and down on the waves, so that she could look into the cabin; but the ship got more and more way on, sail after sail was filled by the wind, the waves grew stronger, great clouds gathered, and it lightened in the distance. Oh, there was going to be a fearful storm! and soon the sailors had to shorten sail. The great ship rocked and rolled as she dashed over the angry sea, the black waves rose like mountains, high enough to overwhelm her, but she dived like a swan through them and rose again and again on their towering crests. The little mermaid thought it a most amusing race, but not so the sailors. The ship creaked and groaned, the mighty timbers bulged and bent under the heavy blows, the water broke over the decks, snapping the mainmast like a reed; she heeled over on her side and the water rushed into the hold.

Now the little mermaid saw that they were in danger and she had for her own sake to beware of the floating beams and wreckage. One moment it was so pitch dark that she could not see at all, but when the lightning flashed it became so light that she could see all on board.

Every man was looking out for his own safety as best he could, but she more particularly followed the young prince with her eyes, and when the ship went down she saw him sink in the deep sea. At first she was quite delighted, for now he was coming to be with her, but then she remembered that human beings could not live under water, and that only if he were dead could he go to her father's palace. No! he must not die; so she swam towards him all among the drifting beams and planks, quite forgetting that they might crush her. She dived deep down under the water, and came up again through the waves, and at last reached the young prince just as he was becoming unable to swim any further in the stormy sea. His limbs were numbed, his beautiful eyes were closing, and he must have died if the little mermaid had not come to the rescue. She held his head above the water and let the waves drive them whithersoever they would.

By daybreak all the storm was over, of the ship not a trace was to be seen; the sun rose from the water in radiant brilliance and his rosy beams seemed to cast a glow of life into the prince's cheeks, but his eyes remained closed. The mermaid kissed his fair brow, and stroked back the dripping hair; it seemed to her that he was like the marble statue in her little garden, she kissed him again and longed that he might live.

At last she saw dry land before her, high blue mountains on whose summits the white snow glistened as if a flock of swans had settled there; down by the shore were beautiful green woods, and in the foreground a church or temple, she did not quite know which, but it was a building of some sort. Lemon and orange trees grew in the garden and lofty palms stood by the gate. At this point the sea formed a little bay where the water was quite calm, but very deep, right up to the cliffs; at their foot was a strip of fine white sand to which she swam with the beautiful prince, and laid him down on it, taking great care that his head should rest high up in the warm sunshine.

The bells now began to ring in the great white building

and a number of young maidens came into the garden. Then the little mermaid swam further off behind some high rocks and covered her hair and breast with foam, so that no one should see her little face, and then she watched to see who would discover the poor prince.

It was not long before one of the maidens came up to him; at first she seemed quite frightened, but only for a moment, and then she fetched several others, and the mermaid saw that the prince was coming to life, and that he smiled at all those around him, but he never smiled at her; you see he did not know that she had saved him; she felt so sad that when he was led away into the great building she dived sorrowfully into the water and made her way home to her father's palace.

Always silent and thoughtful, she became more so now than ever. Her sisters often asked her what she had seen on her first visit to the surface, but she never would tell them anything.

Many an evening and many a morning she would rise to the place where she had left the prince. She saw the fruit in the garden ripen, and then gathered, she saw the snow melt on the mountain-tops, but she never saw the prince, so she always went home still sadder than before. At home her only consolation was to sit in her little garden with her arms twined round the handsome marble statue which reminded her of the prince. It was all in gloomy shade now, as she had ceased to tend her flowers and the garden had become a neglected wilderness of long stalks and leaves entangled with the branches of the tree.

At last she could not bear it any longer, so she told one of her sisters, and from her it soon spread to the others, but to no one else except to one or two other mermaids who only told their dearest friends. One of these knew all about the prince, she had also seen the festivities on the ship; she knew where he came from and where his kingdom was situated.

"Come, little sister!" said the other princesses, and, throwing their arms round each other's shoulders, they rose from the water in a long line, just in front of the prince's palace.

It was built of light yellow glistening stone, with great marble staircases, one of which led into the garden. Magnificent gilded cupolas rose above the roof, and the spaces between the columns which encircled the building were filled with lifelike marble statues. Through the clear glass of the lofty windows you could see gorgeous halls adorned with costly silken hangings, and the pictures on the walls were a sight worth seeing. In the midst of the central hall a large fountain played, throwing its jets of spray upwards to a glass dome in the roof, through which the sunbeams lighted up the water and the beautiful plants which grew in the great basin.

She knew now where he lived and often used to go there in the evenings and by night over the water; she swam much nearer the land than any of the others dared, she even ventured right up the narrow channel under the splendid marble terrace which threw a long shadow over the water. She used to sit here looking at the young prince who thought he was quite alone in the clear moonlight.

She saw him many an evening sailing about in his beautiful boat, with flags waving and music playing, she used to peep through the green rushes, and if the wind happened to catch her long silvery veil and anyone saw it, they only thought it was a swan flapping its wings.

Many a night she heard the fishermen, who were fishing by torchlight, talking over the good deeds of the young prince; and she was happy to think that she had saved his life when he was drifting about on the waves, half dead, and she could not forget how closely his head had pressed her breast, and how passionately she had kissed him; but he knew nothing of all this, and never saw her even in his dreams.

She became fonder and fonder of mankind, and longed more and more to be able to live among them; their world seemed so infinitely bigger than hers; with their ships they could scour the ocean, they could ascend the mountains high above the clouds, and their wooded, grass-grown lands extended further than her eye could reach. There was so much that she wanted to know, but her sisters could not give an answer to all her questions, so she asked her old grandmother who knew the upper world well, and rightly called it the country above the sea.

"If men are not drowned," asked the little mermaid, "do they live forever, do they not die as we do down here in the sea?"

"Yes," said the old lady, "they have to die too, and their lifetime is even shorter than ours. We may live here for three hundred years, but when we cease to exist, we become mere foam on the water and do not have so much as a grave among our dear ones. We have no immortal souls, we have no future life, we are just like the green seaweed, which, once cut down, can never revive again! Men, on the other hand, have a soul which lives forever, lives after the body has become dust; it rises through the clear air, up to the shining stars! Just as we rise from the water to see the land of mortals, so they rise up to unknown beautiful regions which we shall never see."

"Why have we no immortal souls?" asked the little mermaid sadly. "I would give all my three hundred years to be a human being for one day, and afterwards to have a share in the heavenly kingdom."

"You must not be thinking about that," said the grandmother; "we are much better off and happier than human beings."

"Then I shall have to die and to float as foam on the water, and never hear the music of the waves or see the beautiful flowers or the red sun! Is there nothing I can do to gain an immortal soul?"

"No," said the grandmother, "only if a human being so loved you, that you were more to him than father or mother, if all his thoughts and all his love were so centered in you that he would let the priest join your hands and would vow to be faithful to you here, and to all eternity; then your body would become infused with his soul.

Thus and only thus, could you gain a share in the felicity of mankind. He would give you a soul while yet keeping his own. But that can never happen! That which is your greatest beauty in the sea, your fish's tail, is thought hideous up on earth, so little do they understand about it; to be pretty there you must have two clumsy supports which they call legs!"

Then the little mermaid sighed and looked sadly at her fish's tail.

"Let us be happy," said the grandmother, "we will hop and skip during our three hundred years of life, it is surely a long enough time, and after it is over, we shall rest all the better in our graves. There is to be a court ball to-night."

This was a much more splendid affair than we ever see on earth. The walls and the ceiling of the great ballroom were of thick but transparent glass. Several hundreds of colossal mussel shells, rose-red and grass-green, were ranged in order round the sides holding blue lights, which illuminated the whole room and shone through the walls, so that the sea outside was quite lit up. You could see countless fish, great and small, swimming towards the glass walls, some with shining scales of crimson hue, while others were golden and silvery. In the middle of the room was a broad stream of running water, and on this the mermaids and mermen danced to their own beautiful singing. No earthly beings have such lovely voices. The little mermaid sang more sweetly than any of them and they all applauded her. For a moment she felt glad at heart, for she knew that she had the finest voice either in the sea or on land. But she soon began to think again about the upper world, she could not forget the handsome prince and her sorrow in not possessing, like him, an immortal soul. Therefore she stole out of her father's palace, and while all within was joy and merriment, she sat sadly in her little garden. Suddenly she heard the sound of a horn through the water, and she thought, "Now he is out sailing up there; he whom I love more than father or mother, he to whom my thoughts cling and to whose hands I am ready to commit the happiness of my life. I will dare anything to win him and to gain an immortal soul! While my sisters are dancing in my father's palace, I will go to the sea witch of whom I have always been very much afraid, she will perhaps be able to advise and help me!"

Thereupon the little mermaid left the garden and went towards the roaring whirlpools at the back of which the witch lived. She had never been that way before; no flowers grew there, no seaweed, only the bare gray sands, stretched towards the whirlpools, which like rushing mill-wheels swirled round, dragging everything that came within reach down to the depths. She had to pass between these boiling eddies to reach the witch's domain, and for a long way the only path led over warm bubbling mud, which the witch called her "peat bog." Her house stood behind this in the midst of a weird forest. All the trees and bushes were polyps, half animal and half plant; they looked like hundred-headed snakes growing out of the sand, the branches were long slimy arms, with tentacles like wriggling worms, every joint of which from the root to the outermost tip was in constant motion. They wound themselves tightly round whatever they could lay hold of and never let it escape. The little mermaid standing outside was quite frightened, her heart beat fast with terror and she nearly turned back, but then she remembered the prince and the immortal soul of mankind and took courage. She bound her long flowing hair tightly round her head, so that the polyps should not seize her by it, folded her hands over her breast, and darted like a fish through the water, in between the hideous polyps which stretched out their sensitive arms and tentacles towards her. She could see that every one of them had something or other, which they had grasped with their hundred arms, and which they held as if in iron bands. The bleached bones of men who had perished at sea and sunk below peeped forth from the arms of some, while others clutched rudders and sea chests, or the skeleton of some land animal; and most horrible of all, a little mermaid whom they had caught and suffocated. Then she came to a large opening in the wood where the ground was all slimy, and where some huge fat water snakes were gamboling about. In the middle of this opening was a house built of the bones of the wrecked; there sat the witch, letting a toad eat out of her mouth, just as mortals let a little canary eat sugar. She called the hideous water snakes her little chickens, and allowed them to crawl about on her unsightly bosom.

"I know very well what you have come here for," said the witch. "It is very foolish of you! All the same you shall have your way, because it will lead you into misfortune, my fine princess. You want to get rid of your fish's tail, and instead to have two stumps to walk about upon like human beings, so that the young prince may fall in love with you, and that you may win him and an immortal soul." Saying this, she gave such a loud hideous laugh that the toad and snakes fell to the ground and wriggled about there.

"You are just in the nick of time," said the witch; "after sunrise to-morrow I should not be able to help you until another year had run its course. I will make you a potion, and before sunrise you must swim ashore with it, seat yourself on the beach and drink it; then your tail will divide and shrivel up to what men call beautiful legs, but it hurts, it is as if a sharp sword were running through you. All who see you will say that you are the most beautiful child of man they have ever seen. You will keep your gliding gait, no dancer will rival you, but every step you take will be as if you were treading upon sharp knives, so sharp as to draw blood. If you are willing to suffer all this I am ready to help you!"

"Yes!" said the little princess with a trembling voice, thinking of the prince and of winning an undying soul.

"But remember," said the witch, "when once you have received a human form, you can never be a mermaid again, you will never again be able to dive down through the water to your sisters and to your father's palace. And if you do not succeed in winning the prince's love, so that for your sake he will forget father and mother, cleave to you with his whole heart, let the priest join your hands and make you man and wife, you will gain no immortal soul! The first morning after his marriage with another your heart will break, and you will turn into foam of the sea."

"I will do it," said the little mermaid as pale as death.

"But you will have to pay me, too," said the witch, "and it is no trifle that I demand. You have the most beautiful voice of any at the bottom of the sea, and I daresay that you think you will fascinate him with it, but you must give me that voice. I will have the best you possess in return for my precious potion! I have to mingle my own blood with it so as to make it as sharp as a two-edged sword."

"But if you take my voice," said the little mermaid, "what have I left?"

"Your beautiful form," said the witch, "your gliding gait, and your speaking eyes, with these you ought surely to be able to bewitch a human heart. Well! have you lost courage? Put out your little tongue and I will cut it off in payment for the powerful draught."

"Let it be done," said the little mermaid, and the witch put on her cauldron to brew the magic potion. "There is nothing like cleanliness," said she, as she scoured the pot with a bundle of snakes; then she punctured her breast and let the black blood drop into the cauldron, and the steam took the most weird shape, enough to frighten any-one. Every moment the witch threw new ingredients into the pot, and when it boiled the bubbling was like the sound of crocodiles weeping. At last the potion was ready and it looked like the clearest water.

"There it is," said the witch, and thereupon she cut off the tongue of the little mermaid, who was dumb now and could neither sing nor speak.

"If the polyps should seize you, when you go back

through my wood," said the witch, "just drop a single drop of this liquid on them, and their arms and fingers will burst into a thousand pieces." But the little mermaid had no need to do this, for at the mere sight of the bright liquid which sparkled in her hand like a shining star, they drew back in terror. So she soon got past the wood, the bog, and the eddying whirlpools.

She saw her father's palace, the lights were all out in the great ballroom, and no doubt all the household was asleep, but she did not dare to go in now that she was dumb and about to leave her home forever. She felt as if her heart would break with grief. She stole into the garden and plucked a flower from each of her sister's plots, wafted with her hand countless kisses towards the palace, and then rose up through the dark blue water.

The sun had not risen when she came in sight of the prince's palace and landed at the beautiful marble steps. The moon was shining bright and clear. The little mermaid drank the burning, stinging draught, and it was like a sharp, two-edged sword running through her tender frame; she fainted away and lay as if she were dead. When the sun rose on the sea she woke up and became conscious of a sharp pang, but just in front of her stood the handsome young prince, fixing his coal black eyes on her; she saw that her fish's tail was gone, and that she had the prettiest little white legs any maiden could desire, but she was quite naked, so she wrapped her long thick hair around her. The prince asked who she was and how she came there; she looked at him tenderly and with a sad expression in her dark blue eyes, but could not speak. Then he took her by the hand and led her into the palace. Every step she took was, as the witch had warned her beforehand, as if she were treading on sharp knives and spikes but she bore it gladly; led by the prince she moved as lightly as a bubble, and he and everyone else marveled at her graceful gliding gait.

Clothed in the costliest silks and muslins she was the greatest beauty in the palace, but she was dumb and could neither sing nor speak. Beautiful slaves clad in silks and gold came forward and sang to the prince and his royal parents; one of them sang better than all the others, and the prince clapped his hands and smiled at her; that made the little mermaid very sad, for she knew that she used to sing far better herself. She thought, "Oh! if he only knew that for the sake of being with him I had given up my voice forever!" Now the slaves began to dance, graceful undulating dances to enchanting music; thereupon the little mermaid lifting her beautiful white arms and raising herself on tiptoe glided on the floor with a grace which none of the other dancers had yet attained. With every motion her grace and beauty became more apparent, and her eyes appealed more deeply to the heart than the songs of the slaves. Everyone was delighted with it, especially the prince, who called her his foundling, and she danced on and on, notwithstanding that every time her foot touched the ground it was like treading on sharp knives. The prince said that she should always be near him, and she was allowed to sleep outside his door on a velvet cushion.

He had a man's dress made for her, so that she could ride about with him. They used to ride through scented woods, where the green branches brushed her shoulders, and little birds sang among the fresh leaves. She climbed up the highest mountains with the prince, and although her delicate feet bled so that others saw it, she only laughed and followed him until they saw the clouds sailing below them like a flock of birds, taking flight to distant lands.

At home in the prince's palace, when at night the others were asleep, she used to go out on to the marble steps; it cooled her burning feet to stand in the cold sea water, and at such times she used to think of those she had left in the deep.

One night her sisters came arm in arm; they sang so sorrowfully as they swam on the water that she beckoned to them and they recognized her, and told her how she had grieved them all. After that they visited her every night, and one night she saw, a long way out, her old grandmother (who for many years had not been above the water), and the Merman King with his crown on his head; they stretched out their hands towards her, but did not venture so close to land as her sisters.

Day by day she became dearer to the prince, he loved her as one loves a good sweet child, but it never entered his head to make her his queen; yet unless she became his wife she would never win an everlasting soul, but on his wedding morning would turn to sea foam.

"Am I not dearer to you than any of them?" the little mermaid's eyes seemed to say when he took her in his arms and kissed her beautiful brow.

"Yes, you are the dearest one to me," said the prince, "for you have the best heart of them all, and you are fondest of me; you are also like a young girl I once saw, but whom I never expect to see again. I was on board a ship which was wrecked, I was driven on shore by the waves close to a holy Temple where several young girls were ministering at a service; the youngest of them found me on the beach and saved my life; I saw her but twice. She was the only person I could love in this world, but you are like her, you almost drive her image out of my heart. She belongs to the holy Temple, and therefore by good fortune you have been sent to me, we will never part!"

"Alas! he does not know that it was I who saved his life," thought the little mermaid. "I bore him over the sea to the wood, where the Temple stands. I sat behind the foam and watched to see if anyone would come. I saw the pretty girl he loves better than me." And the mermaid heaved a bitter sigh, for she could not weep.

"The girl belongs to the holy Temple, he has said, she will never return to the world, they will never meet again, I am here with him, I see him every day. Yes! I will tend him, love him, and give up my life to him."

But now the rumor ran that the prince was to be married to the beautiful daughter of a neighboring king, and for that reason was fitting out a splendid ship. It was given out that the prince was going on a voyage to see the adjoining countries, but it was without doubt to see the king's daughter; he was to have a great suite with him, but the little mermaid shook her head and laughed; she knew the prince's intentions much better than any of the others. "I must take this voyage," he had said to her; "I must go and see the beautiful princess; my parents demand that, but they will never force me to bring her home as my bride; I can never love her! She will not be like the lovely girl in the Temple whom you resemble. If ever I had to choose a bride it would sooner be you with your speaking eyes, my sweet, dumb foundling!" And he kissed her rosy mouth, played with her long hair, and laid his head upon her heart, which already dreamed of human joys and an immortal soul.

"You are not frightened of the sea, I suppose, my dumb child?" he said, as they stood on the proud ship which was to carry them to the country of the neighboring king; and he told her about storms and calms, about curious fish in the deep, and the marvels seen by divers; and she smiled at his tales, for she knew all about the bottom of the sea much better than anyone else.

At night, in the moonlight, when all were asleep, except the steersman who stood at the helm, she sat at the side of the ship trying to pierce the clear water with her eyes, and fancied she saw her father's palace, and above it her old grandmother with her silver crown on her head, looking up through the cross currents towards the keel of the ship. Then her sisters rose above the water, they gazed sadly at her, wringing their white hands; she beckoned to them, smiled, and was about to tell them that all was going well and happily with her, when the cabin boy approached, and the sisters dived down, but he supposed that the white objects he had seen were nothing but flakes of foam.

The next morning the ship entered the harbor of the neighboring king's magnificent city. The church bells rang and trumpets were sounded from every lofty tower, while the soldiers paraded with flags flying and glittering bayonets. There was a fête every day, there was a succession of balls, and receptions followed one after the other, but the princess was not yet present, she was being brought up a long way off, in a holy Temple they said, and was learning all the royal virtues. At last she came. The little mermaid stood eager to see her beauty, she was obliged to confess that a lovelier creature she had never beheld. Her complexion was exquisitely pure and delicate, and her trustful eyes of the deepest blue shone through their dark lashes.

"It is you," said the prince, "you who saved me when I lay almost lifeless on the beach?" and he clasped his blushing bride to his heart. "Oh! I am too happy!" he exclaimed to the little mermaid.

"A greater joy than I had dared to hope for has come to pass. You will rejoice at my joy, for you love me better than anyone." Then the little mermaid kissed his hand, and felt as if her heart were broken already.

His wedding morn would bring death to her and change her to foam.

All the church bells pealed and heralds rode through the town proclaiming the nuptials. Upon every altar throughout the land fragrant oil was burned in costly silver lamps. Amidst the swinging of censers by the priests, the bride and bridegroom joined hands and received the bishop's blessing. The little mermaid dressed in silk and gold stood holding the bride's train, but her ears were deaf to the festal strains, her eyes saw nothing of the sacred ceremony, she was thinking of her coming death and of all that she had lost in this world.

That same evening the bride and bridegroom embarked, amidst the roar of cannon and the waving of banners. A royal tent of purple and gold softly cushioned was raised amidships where the bridal pair were to repose during the cool night.

The sails swelled in the wind and the ship skimmed

lightly and almost without motion over the transparent sea.

At dusk lanterns of many colors were lighted and the sailors danced merrily on deck. The little mermaid could not help thinking of the first time she came up from the sea and saw the same splendor and gayety; and she now threw herself among the dancers, whirling, as a swallow skims through the air when pursued. The onlookers cheered her in amazement, never had she danced so divinely; her delicate feet pained her as if they were cut with knives, but she did not feel it, for the pain at her heart was much sharper. She knew that it was the last night that she would breathe the same air as he, and would look upon the mighty deep, and the blue starry heavens; an endless night without thought and without dreams awaited her, who neither had a soul, nor could win one. The joy and revelry on board lasted till long past midnight, she went on laughing and dancing with the thought of death all the time in her heart. The prince caressed his lovely bride and she played with his raven locks, and with their arms entwined they retired to the gorgeous tent. All became hushed and still on board the ship, only the steersman stood at the helm, the little mermaid laid her white arms on the gunwale and looked eastwards for the pink tinted dawn; the first sunbeam, she knew, would be her death. Then she saw her sisters rise from the water, they were as pale as she was, their beautiful long hair no longer floated on the breeze, for it had been cut off.

"We have given it to the witch to obtain her help, so that you may not die to-night! she has given us a knife, here it is, look how sharp it is! Before the sun rises, you must plunge it into the prince's heart, and when his warm blood sprinkles your feet they will join together and grow into a tail, and you will once more be a mermaid; you will be able to come down into the water to us, and to live out your three hundred years before you are turned into dead, salt, sea-foam. Make haste! you or he must die before sunrise! Our old grandmother is so full of grief that her white hair has fallen off as ours fell under the witch's scissors. Slay the prince and come back to us! Quick! Quick! do you not see the rosy streak in the sky? In a few moments the sun will rise and then you must die!" Saying this they heaved a wondrous deep sigh and sank among the waves.

The little mermaid drew aside the purple curtain from the tent and looked at the beautiful bride asleep with her head on the prince's breast; she bent over him and kissed his fair brow, looked at the sky where the dawn was spreading fast; looked at the sharp knife, and again fixed her eyes on the prince who, in his dream called his bride by name, yes she alone was in his thoughts!—For a moment the knife quivered in her grasp, then she threw it far out among the waves now rosy in the morning light and where it fell the water bubbled up like drops of blood.

Once more she looked at the prince, with her eyes already dimmed by death, then dashed overboard and fell, her body dissolving into foam.

Now the sun rose from the sea and with its kindly beams warmed the deadly cold foam, so that the little mermaid did not feel the chill of death. She saw the bright sun and above her floated hundreds of beauteous ethereal beings through which she could see the white ship and the rosy heavens, their voices were melodious but so spirit-like that no human ear could hear them, any more than an earthly eye could see their forms. Light as bubbles they floated through the air without the aid of wings. The little mermaid perceived that she had a form like theirs, it gradually took shape out of the foam. "To whom am I coming?" said she, and her voice sounded like that of the other beings, so unearthly in its beauty that no music of ours could reproduce it.

"To the daughters of the air!" answered the others; "a mermaid has no undying soul, and can never gain one without winning the love of a human being. Her eternal life must depend upon an unknown power. Nor have the daughters of the air an everlasting soul, but by their own good deeds they may create one for themselves. We fly to the tropics where mankind is the victim of hot and pestilent winds, there we bring cooling breezes. We diffuse the scent of flowers all around, and bring refreshment and healing in our train. When, for three hundred years, we have labored to do all the good in our power we gain an undying soul and take a part in the everlasting joys of mankind. You, poor little mermaid, have with your whole heart, struggled for the same thing as we have struggled for. You have suffered and endured, raised yourself to the spirit world of the air; and now, by your own good deeds you may, in the course of three hundred years, work out for yourself an undying soul."

Then the little mermaid lifted her transparent arms towards God's sun, and for the first time shed tears.

On board ship all was again life and bustle, she saw the prince with his lovely bride searching for her, they looked sadly at the bubbling foam, as if they knew that she had thrown herself into the waves. Unseen she kissed the bride on her brow, smiled at the prince and rose aloft with the other spirits of the air to the rosy clouds which sailed above.

"In three hundred years we shall thus float into Paradise."

"We might reach it sooner," whispered one. "Unseen we flit into those homes of men where there are children, and for every day that we find a good child who gives pleasure to its parents and deserves their love, God shortens our time of probation. The child does not know when we fly through the room, and when we smile with pleasure at it, one year of our three hundred is taken away. But if we see a naughty or badly disposed child, we cannot help shedding tears of sorrow, and every tear adds a day to the time of our probation."

The Tinder Box

A SOLDIER came marching along the highroad. One, two! One, two! He had his knapsack on his back and his sword at his side, for he had been to the wars and he was on his way home now. He met an old witch on the road. She was so ugly, her lower lip hung right down on to her chin.

She said, "Good-evening, soldier! What a nice sword you've got, and such a big knapsack; you are a real soldier! You shall have as much money as ever you like!"

"Thank you kindly, you old witch!" said the soldier.

"Do you see that big tree!" said the witch, pointing to a tree close by. "It is hollow inside! Climb up to the top and you will see a hole into which you can let yourself down, right down under the tree! I will tie a rope round your waist so that I can haul you up again when you call!"

"What am I to do down under that tree?" asked the soldier.

"Fetch money!" said the witch. "You must know that when you get down to the bottom of the tree you will find yourself in a wide passage; it's quite light there, for there are over a hundred blazing lamps. You will see three doors which you can open, for the keys are there. If you go into the first room you will see a big box in the middle of the floor. A dog is sitting on top of it, and he has eyes as big as saucers, but you needn't mind that. I will give you my blue checked apron, which you can spread out on the floor; then go quickly forward, take up the dog and put him on my apron, open the box and take out as much money as ever you like. It is all copper, but if you like silver better, go into the next room. There you will find a dog with eyes as big as millstones; but never mind that, put him on my apron and take the money. If you prefer gold you can have it too, and as much as you can carry, if you go into the third room. But the dog sitting on that box has eyes each as big as the Round Tower. He is a dog, indeed, as you may imagine! But don't let it trouble you; you only have to put him on to my apron and then he won't hurt you, and you can take as much gold out of the box as you like!"

"That's not so bad!" said the soldier. "But what am I to give you, old witch? For you'll want something, I'll be bound."

"No," said the witch, "not a single penny do I want. I only want you to bring me an old tinder box that my grandmother forgot the last time she was down there!"

"Well! tie the rope round my waist!" said the soldier.

"Here it is," said the witch, "and here is my blue-checked apron."

Then the soldier climbed up the tree, let himself slide down the hollow trunk, and found himself, as the witch had said, in the wide passage where the many hundred lamps were burning.

Now he opened the first door. Ugh! There sat the dog with eyes as big as saucers, staring at him.

"You are a nice fellow!" said the soldier, as he put him on to the witch's apron, and took out as many pennies as he could cram into his pockets. Then he shut the box, and put the dog on top of it again, and went into the next room. Hallo! there sat the dog with eyes as big as millstones.

"You shouldn't stare at me so hard! You might get a pain in your eyes!" Then he put the dog on the apron, but when he saw all the silver in the box he threw away all the coppers and stuffed his pockets and his knapsack with silver. Then he went on into the third room. Oh! how horrible!

that dog really had two big eyes as big as the Round Tower, and they rolled round and round like wheels.

"Good-evening!" said the soldier, saluting, for he had never seen such a dog in his life; but after looking at him for a bit he thought, "That will do," and he lifted him down on to the apron and opened the chest. Preserve us! What a lot of gold! He could buy the whole of Copenhagen with it, and all the sugar pigs from the cake-women, all the tin soldiers, whips and rocking-horses in the world! That was money indeed! Now the soldier threw away all the silver he had filled his pockets and his knapsack with, and put gold in its place. Yes, he crammed all his pockets, his knapsack, his cap and his boots so full that he could hardly walk! Now, he really had got a lot of money. He put the dog back on to the box, shut the door, and shouted up through the tree, "Haul me up, you old witch!"

"Have you got the tinder box?"

"Oh! to be sure!" said the soldier. "I had quite forgotten it." And he went back to fetch it. The witch hauled him up, and there he was, standing on the highroad again with his pockets, boots, knapsack and cap full of gold.

"What do you want the tinder box for?" asked the soldier.

"That's no business of yours," said the witch. "You've got the money. Give me the tinder box!"

"Rubbish!" said the soldier. "Tell me directly what you want with it, or I will draw my sword and cut off your head."

"I won't!" said the witch.

Then the soldier cut off her head. There she lay, but he tied all the money up in her apron, slung it on his back like a pack, put the tinder box in his pocket, and marched off to the town.

It was a beautiful town, and he went straight to the finest hotel, ordered the grandest rooms and all the food he liked best, for he was a rich man, now that he had so much money.

Certainly the servant who had to clean his boots

thought they were very funny old things for such a rich gentleman, but he had not had time yet to buy any new ones; the next day he bought new boots and fine clothes. The soldier now became a fine gentleman, and the people told him all about the grand things in the town, and about their king, and what a lovely princess his daughter was.

"Where is she to be seen?" asked the soldier.

"You can't see her at all!" they all said. "She lives in a great copper castle surrounded with walls and towers. Nobody but the king dare go in and out, for it has been prophesied that she will marry a common soldier, and the king doesn't like that!"

"I should like to see her well enough!" thought the soldier. But there was no way of getting leave for that.

He now led a very merry life, went to theaters, drove about in the King's Park, and gave away a lot of money to the poor people, which was very nice of him; for he remembered how disagreeable it used to be not to have a penny in his pocket. Now he was rich, wore fine clothes, and had a great many friends, who all said what a nice fellow he was—a thorough gentleman—and he liked to be told that.

But as he went on spending money every day and his store was never renewed, he at last found himself with only two pence left. Then he was obliged to move out of his fine rooms. He had to take a tiny little attic up under the roof, clean his own boots, and mend them, himself, with a darning needle. None of his friends went to see him, because there were far too many stairs.

One dark evening, when he had not even enough money to buy a candle with, he suddenly remembered that there was a little bit in the old tinder box he had brought out of the hollow tree, when the witch helped him down. He got out the tinder box with the candle end in it and struck fire. As the sparks flew out from the flint, the door burst open and the dog with eyes as big as saucers, which he had seen down under the tree, stood before him and said, "What does my lord command?"

"By heaven!" said the soldier, "this is a nice kind of tinder box, if I can get whatever I want like this! Get me some money," he said to the dog, and away it went.

It was back in a twinkling with a big bag full of pennies in its mouth.

Now the soldier saw what a treasure he had in the tinder box. If he struck once, the dog which sat on the box of copper came; if he struck twice, the dog on the silver box came; and if he struck three times, the one from the box of gold.

He now moved down to the grand rooms and got his fine clothes again, and then all his friends knew him once more and liked him as much as ever.

Then he began to think: After all, it's a curious thing that no man can get a sight of the princess! Everyone says she is so beautiful! But what is the good of that, when she always has to be shut up in that big copper palace with all the towers. Can I not somehow manage to see her? Where is my tinder box? Then he struck the flint, and, whisk, came the dog with eyes as big as saucers.

"It certainly is the middle of the night," said the soldier, "but I am very anxious to see the princess, if only for a single moment."

The dog was out of the door in an instant, and before the soldier had time to think about it, he was back again with the princess. There she was, fast asleep on the dog's back, and she was so lovely that anybody could see that she must be a real princess! The soldier could not help it; he was obliged to kiss her, for he was a true soldier.

Then the dog ran back again with the princess, but in the morning when the king and queen were having breakfast, the princess said that she had had such a wonderful dream about a dog and a soldier. She had ridden on the dog's back, and the soldier had kissed her.

"That's a pretty tale," said the queen.

After this an old lady-in-waiting had to sit by her bed at night to see if this was really a dream.

The soldier longed so intensely to see the princess

again that at night the dog came to fetch her. He took her up and ran off with her as fast as he could, but the old lady-in-waiting put on her galoshes and ran just as fast behind them. When she saw that they disappeared into a large house, she thought, now I know where it is, and made a big cross with chalk on the gate. Then she went home and lay down, and presently the dog came back, too, with the princess. When the dog saw that there was a cross on the gate, he took a bit of chalk, too, and made crosses on all the gates in the town. Now this was very clever of him, for the lady-in-waiting could not possibly find the gate when there were crosses on all the gates.

Early next morning the king, and queen, the lady-in-waiting, and all the court officials went to see where the princess had been.

"There it is," said the king, when he saw the first door with the cross on it.

"No, my dear husband, it is there," said the queen, who saw another door with a cross on it.

"But there is one, and there is another!" they all cried out.

They soon saw that it was hopeless to try and find it.

Now the queen was a very clever woman; she knew more than how to drive in a chariot. She took her big gold scissors and cut up a large piece of silk into small pieces, and made a pretty little bag, which she filled with fine grains of buckwheat. She then tied it on the back of the princess, and when that was done, she cut a little hole in the bag, so that the grains could drop out all the way wherever the princess went.

At night the dog came again, took the princess on his back, and ran off with her to the soldier, who was so fond of her that he longed to be a prince, so that he might have her for his wife.

The dog never noticed how the grain dropped out all along the road from the palace to the soldier's window, where he ran up the wall with the princess.

In the morning the king and queen easily saw where

their daughter had been, and they seized the soldier and threw him into the dungeons.

There he lay! Oh, how dark and tiresome it was, and then one day they said to him, "Tomorrow you are to be hanged." It was not amusing to be told that, especially as he had left his tinder box behind him at the hotel.

In the morning he could see through the bars in the little window that people were hurrying out of the town to see him hanged. He heard the drums and saw the soldiers go marching along. All the world was going; among them was a shoemaker's boy in his leather apron and slippers. He was in such a hurry that he lost one of his slippers, and it fell close under the soldier's window where he was peeping through the bars. "I say, you boy! Don't be in such a hurry," said the soldier to him. "Nothing will happen till I get there! But if you will run to the house where I used to live, and fetch me my tinder box, you shall have a penny!"

The boy was only too glad to have the penny, and tore off to get the tinder box, gave it to the soldier, and—yes, now we shall hear!

Outside the town a high scaffold had been raised, and the soldiers were drawn up round about it, as well as crowds of townspeople. The king and the queen sat upon a beautiful throne exactly opposite the judge and all the councillors.

The soldier mounted the ladder, but when they were about to put the rope round his neck, he said that, before undergoing his punishment, a criminal was always allowed the gratification of a harmless wish, and he wanted very much to smoke a pipe, as it would be his last pipe in this world.

The king could not deny him this, so the soldier took out his tinder box and struck fire, once, twice, three times, and there were all the dogs. The one with eyes like saucers, the one with eyes like millstones, and the one whose eyes were as big as the Round Tower.

"Help me! Save me from being hanged!" cried the soldier.

And then the dogs rushed at the soldiers and the councillors; they took one by the legs, and another by the nose, and threw them up many fathoms into the air; and when they fell down, they were all broken to pieces.

"I won't!" cried the king, but the biggest dog took both him and the queen and threw them after all the others. Then the soldiers became alarmed, and the people shouted, "Oh! good soldier, you shall be our king and marry the beautiful princess!"

So they conducted the soldier to the king's chariot, and all three dogs danced along in front of him and shouted "Hurrah!" The boys all put their fingers in their mouths and whistled, and the soldiers presented arms. The princess came out of the copper palace and became queen, which pleased her very much. The wedding took place in a week, and the dogs all had seats at the table, where they sat staring with all their eyes.

Great Claus and Little Claus

IN a village there once lived two men of the self-same name. They were both called Claus, but one of them had four horses, and the other only had one; so to distinguish them people called the owner of the four horses "Great Claus," and he who had only one "Little Claus." Now I shall tell you what happened to them, for this is a true story.

Throughout the week Little Claus was obliged to plow for Great Claus, and to lend him his one horse; but once a week, on Sunday, Great Claus lent him all his four horses.

"Hurrah!" How Little Claus would smack his whip over all five, for they were as good as his own on that one day.

The sun shone brightly and the church bells rang merrily as the people passed by, dressed in their best, with their prayer-books under their arms. They were going to hear the parson preach. They looked at Little Claus plowing with his five horses, and he was so proud that he smacked his whip and said, "Gee-up, my five horses."

"You mustn't say that," said Great Claus, "for only one of them is yours."

But Little Claus soon forgot what he ought not to say, and when anyone passed, he would call out, "Gee-up, my five horses."

"I must really beg you not to say that again," said Great Claus, "for if you do, I shall hit your horse on the head, so that he will drop down dead on the spot, and there will be an end of him."

"I promise you I will not say it again," said the other; but as soon as anybody came by nodding to him, and wishing him "Good-day," he was so pleased, and thought how grand it was to have five horses plowing in his field, that he cried out again, "Gee-up, all my horses!"

"I'll gee-up your horses for you," said Great Claus, and seizing the tethering mallet he struck Little Claus' one horse on the head, and it fell down dead.

"Oh, now I have no horse at all," said Little Claus, weeping. But after a long while he flayed the dead horse, and hung up the skin in the wind to dry.

Then he put the dry skin into a bag, and hanging it over his shoulder went off to the next town to sell it. But he had a long way to go, and had to pass through a dark and gloomy forest.

Presently a storm arose, and he lost his way; and before he discovered the right path evening was drawing on, and it was still a long way to the town, and too far to return home before nightfall.

Near the road stood a large farmhouse. The shutters outside the windows were closed, but lights shone through the crevices and at the top. "They might let me stay here for the night," thought Little Claus, so he went up to the door and knocked. The farmer's wife opened the door, but when she heard what he wanted, she told him to go away; her husband was not at home, and she could not let any strangers in.

"Then I shall have to lie out here," said Little Claus to himself as the farmer's wife shut the door in his face.

Close to the farmhouse stood a large haystack, and between it and the house there was a small shed with a thatched roof. "I can lie up there," said Little Claus, looking at the roof. "It will make a famous bed, but I hope the stork won't fly down and bite my legs." A live stork was standing up there who had his nest on the roof.

So Little Claus climbed on the roof of the shed, and as he turned about to make himself comfortable he discovered that the wooden shutters did not reach to the top of the windows, so that he could see into the room, in which a large table was laid out, with wine, roast meat, and a splendid fish.

The farmer's wife and the sexton were sitting at table together. Nobody else was there. She was filling his glass and helping him plentifully to fish.

"If only I could have some, too," thought Little Claus, and then, as he stretched out his neck towards the window, he spied a beautiful, large cake—indeed they had a glorious feast before them.

At that moment he heard someone riding down the road towards the farm. It was the farmer coming home.

He was a good man, but he had one very strange prejudice—he could not bear the sight of a sexton. If he happened to see one, he would get into a terrible rage. In consequence of this dislike, the sexton had gone to visit the farmer's wife during her husband's absence from home, and the good woman had put before him the best of everything she had in the house to eat.

When they heard the farmer, they were dreadfully frightened, and the woman made the sexton creep into a large chest which stood in a corner. He went at once, for he was well aware of the poor man's aversion to the sight of a sexton. The woman then quickly hid all the nice things and the wine in the oven, because if her husband had seen it he would have asked questions.

"Oh, dear!" sighed Little Claus, on the roof, when he saw the food disappearing.

"Is there anyone up there?" asked the farmer, peering up at Little Claus. "What are you doing up there? You had better come into the house."

Then Little Claus told him how he had lost his way, and asked if he might have shelter for the night.

"Certainly," said the farmer; "but the first thing is to have something to eat."

The woman received them both very kindly, laid the table, and gave them a large bowl of porridge. The farmer was hungry, and ate it with a good appetite; but Little

Claus could not help thinking of the good roast meat, the fish and the cake, which he knew were hidden in the oven.

He put his sack with the hide in it under the table by his feet, for, as we remember, he was on his way to the town to sell it. He did not fancy the porridge, so he trod on the sack and made the dried hide squeak quite loudly.

"Hush!" said Little Claus to his sack, at the same time treading on it again, so that it squeaked louder than ever.

"What on earth have you got in your sack?" asked the farmer again.

"Oh, it's a Goblin," said Little Claus; "he says we needn't eat the porridge, for he has charmed the oven full of roast meat and fish and cake."

"What do you say!" said the farmer, opening the oven door with all speed, and seeing the nice things the woman had hidden, but which her husband thought the Goblin had produced for their special benefit.

The woman dared not say anything, but put the food before them, and then they both made a hearty meal of the fish, the meat and the cake.

Then Little Claus trod on the skin and made it squeak again.

"What does he say now?" asked the farmer.

"He says," answered Little Claus, "that he has also charmed three bottles of wine into the oven for us."

So the woman had to bring out the wine too, and the farmer drank it and became merry. Wouldn't he like to have a Goblin, like the one in Little Claus' sack, for himself?

"Can he charm out the Devil?" asked the farmer. "I shouldn't mind seeing him, now that I am in such a merry mood."

"Oh, yes!" said Little Claus; "my Goblin can do everything that we ask him. Can't you?" he asked, trampling up the sack till it squeaked louder than ever. "Do you hear what I say? But the Devil is so ugly, you'd better not see him."

"Oh! I'm not a bit frightened. Whatever does he look like?"

"Well, he will show himself in the image of a sexton."

"Oh, dear!" said the farmer; "that's bad! I must tell you that I can't bear to see a sexton! However, it doesn't matter! I shall know it's only the Devil, and then I sha'n't mind so much! Now, my courage is up! But he mustn't come too close."

"I'll ask my Goblin about it," said Little Claus, treading on the bag and putting his ear close to it.

"What does he say?"

"He says you can go along and open the chest in the corner, and there you'll see the Devil moping in the dark; but hold the lid tight so that he doesn't get out."

"Will you help me to hold it?" asked the farmer, going along to the chest where the woman had hidden the real sexton, who was shivering with fright.

The farmer lifted up the lid a wee little bit and peeped in. "Ha!" he shrieked, and sprang back. "Yes, I saw him, and he looked just exactly like our sexton! It was a horrible sight."

They had to have a drink after this, and there they sat drinking till far into the night.

"You must sell me that Goblin," said the farmer. "You may ask what you like for him! I will give you a bushel of money for him."

"No, I can't do that," said Little Claus; "you must remember how useful my Goblin is to me."

"Oh, but I should so like to have him," said the farmer, and he went on begging for him.

"Well," said Little Claus at last, "as you have been so kind to me I shall have to give him up. You shall have my Goblin for a bushel of money, but I must have it full to the brim!"

"You shall have it," said the farmer; "but you must take that chest away with you; I won't have it in the house for another hour."

So Little Claus gave his sack with the dried hide in it to

the farmer, and received in return a bushel of money for it, and the measure was full to the brim. The farmer also gave him a large wheelbarrow to take the money and the chest away in.

"Good-by!" said Little Claus, and off he went with his money and the big chest with the sexton in it.

There was a wide and deep river on the other side of the wood, the stream was so strong that it was almost impossible to swim against it. A large new bridge had been built across it, and when they got into the very middle of it, Little Claus said quite loud, so that the sexton would hear him—

"What am I to do with this stupid old chest? it might be full of paving stones, it's so heavy! I am quite tired of wheeling it along; I'll just throw it into the river. If it floats down the river to my house, well and good, and if it doesn't, I sha'n't care."

Then he took hold of the chest and raised it up a bit, as if he was about to throw it into the river.

"No, no! let it be!" shouted the sexton. "Let me get out!"

"Hullo!" said Little Claus, pretending to be frightened. "Why, he's still inside it, then I must throw it into the river to drown him."

"Oh no, oh no!" shouted the sexton. "I'll give you a bushel full of money if you'll let me out!"

"Oh, that's another matter," said Little Claus, opening the chest. The sexton crept out at once and pushed the empty chest into the water, and then went home and gave Little Claus a whole bushel of money.

"I got a pretty fair price for that horse I must admit!" said he to himself when he got home to his own room and turned the money out of the wheelbarrow into a heap on the floor. "What a rage Great Claus will be in when he discovers how rich I am become through my one horse, but I won't tell him straight out about it." So he sent a boy to Great Claus to borrow a bushel measure.

"What does he want that for!" thought Great Claus, and he rubbed some tallow on the bottom, so that a little of whatever was to be measured might stick to it. So it did, for when the measure came back three new silver three-penny bits were sticking to it.

"What's this?" said Great Claus, and he ran straight along to Little Claus. "Where on earth did you get all that money?"

"Oh, that was for my horse's hide which I sold last night."

"That was well paid, indeed," said Great Claus, and he ran home, took an ax and hit all his four horses on the head. He then flayed them and went off to the town with the hides.

"Skins, skins, who will buy skins?" he shouted up and down the streets.

All the shoemakers and tanners in the town came running up and asked him how much he wanted for them.

"A bushel of money for each," said Great Claus.

"Are you mad?" they all said; "do you imagine we have money by the bushel?"

"Skins, skins, who will buy skins?" he shouted again, and the shoemakers took up their measures and the tanners their leather aprons, and beat Great Claus through the town.

"Skins, skins!" they mocked him. "Yes, we'll give you a rawhide. Out of the town with him!" they shouted, and Great Claus had to hurry off as fast as ever he could go. He had never had such a beating in his life.

"Little Claus shall pay for this!" he said when he got home. "I'll kill him for it."

Little Claus' old grandmother had just died in his house; she certainly had been very cross and unkind to him, but now that she was dead, he felt quite sorry about it. He took the dead woman and put her into his warm bed, to see if he could bring her to life again. He meant her to stay there all night, and he would sit on a chair in the corner; he had slept like that before.

As he sat there in the night, the door opened, and in came Great Claus with his ax, he knew where Little Claus' bed stood, and he went straight up to it and hit the dead grandmother a blow on the forehead, thinking that it was Little Claus.

"Just see if you'll cheat me again after that!" he said, and then he went home again.

"What a bad, wicked man he is," said Little Claus; "he was going to kill me there. What a good thing that poor old granny was dead already, or else he would have killed her."

He now dressed his old grandmother in her best Sunday clothes, borrowed a horse of his neighbor, harnessed it to a cart, and set his grandmother on the back seat, so that she could not fall out when the cart moved. Then he started off through the wood. When the sun rose he was just outside a big inn, and Little Claus drew up his horse and went in to get something to eat.

The landlord was a very, very rich man, and a very good man, but he was fiery-tempered, as if he were made of pepper and tobacco.

"Good-morning!" said he to Little Claus; "you've got your best clothes on very early this morning!"

"Yes," said Little Claus; "I'm going to town with my old grandmother, she's sitting out there in the cart, I can't get her to come in. Won't you take her out a glass of mead? You'll have to shout at her, she's very hard of hearing."

"Yes, she shall have it!" said the innkeeper, and he poured out a large glass of mead which he took out to the dead grandmother in the cart.

"Here is a glass of mead your son has sent!" said the innkeeper, but the dead woman sat quite still and never said a word.

"Don't you hear?" shouted the innkeeper as loud as ever he could; "here is a glass of mead!"

Again he shouted, and then again as loud as ever, but as she did not stir, he got angry and threw the glass of mead in her face, so that the mead ran all over her, and she fell backwards out of the cart, for she was only stuck up and not tied in.

"Now!" shouted Little Claus, as he rushed out of the inn and seized the landlord by the neck, "you have killed my grandmother! Just look, there's a great hole in her forehead!"

"Oh, what a misfortune!" exclaimed the innkeeper, clasping his hands; "that's the consequence of my fiery temper! Good Little Claus, I will give you a bushel of money, and bury your grandmother as if she had been my own, if you will only say nothing about it. If you tell, they will chop my head off, and that is so nasty."

So Little Claus had a whole bushel of money, and the innkeeper buried the old grandmother just as if she had been his own.

When Little Claus got home again with all his money, he immediately sent over his boy to Great Claus to borrow his measure.

"What!" said Great Claus, "is he not dead? I shall have to go and see about it myself!" So he took the measure over to Little Claus himself.

"I say, wherever did you get all that money?" asked he, his eyes round with amazement at what he saw.

"It was my grandmother you killed instead of me!" said Little Claus. "I have sold her and got a bushel of money for her!"

"That was good pay, indeed!" said Great Claus, and he hurried home, took an ax and killed his old grandmother.

He then put her in a cart and drove off to the town with her where the apothecary lived, and asked if he would buy a dead body.

"Who is it, and where did the body come from?" asked the apothecary.

"It is my grandmother, and I have killed her for a bushel of money!" said Great Claus.

"Heaven preserve us!" said the apothecary. "You are talking like a madman; pray don't say such things! You might lose your head!"

And he pointed out to him what a horribly wicked thing he had done, and what a bad man he was. Great Claus was so frightened that he rushed straight out of the shop, jumped into the cart, whipped up his horse and galloped home. The apothecary and everyone else thought he was mad, and so they let him drive off.

"You shall be paid for this!" said Great Claus, when he got out on the highroad. "You shall pay for this, Little Claus!"

As soon as he got home he took the biggest sack he could find, went over to Little Claus and said:

"You have deceived me again! First I killed my horses, and then my old grandmother! It's all your fault, but you sha'n't have the chance of cheating me again!"

Then he took Little Claus by the waist and put him into the sack, put it on his back, and shouted to him:

"I'm going to drown you now!"

It was a long way to go before he came to the river, and Little Claus was not so light to carry. The road passed close by the church in which the organ was playing, and the people were singing beautifully. Great Claus put down the sack with Little Claus in it close by the church door, and thought he would like to go in and hear a psalm before he went any further. Little Claus could not get out of the bag, and all the people were in church, so he went in, too.

"Oh dear, oh dear!" sighed Little Claus in the sack. He turned and twisted, but it was impossible to undo the cord. Just then an old cattle drover with white hair and a tall stick in his hand came along. He had a whole drove of cows and bulls before him. They ran against the sack Little Claus was in, and upset in.

"Oh dear!" sighed Little Claus; "I am so young to be going to the Kingdom of Heaven!"

"And I," said the cattle drover, "am so old and cannot get there yet!"

"Open the sack!" shouted Little Claus. "Get in in place of me, and you will get to heaven directly!"

"That will just suit me," said the cattle drover, undoing the sack for Little Claus, who immediately sprang out.

"You must look after the cattle now," said the old man as he crept into the sack. Little Claus tied it up and walked off, driving the cattle before him.

A little while after Great Claus came out of the church. He took up the sack on his back, and certainly thought it had grown lighter, for the old cattle drover was not more than half the weight of Little Claus. "How light he seems to have got; that must be because I have been to church and said my prayers!" Then he went on to the river, which was both wide and deep, and threw the sack with the old cattle drover in it into the water, shouting as he did so (for he thought it was Little Claus), "Now, you won't cheat me again!" Then he went homewards, but when he reached the crossroads he met Little Claus with his herd of cattle.

"What's the meaning of this?" exclaimed Great Claus. "Didn't I drown you?"

"Yes," said Little Claus, "it's only about half an hour since you threw me into the river!"

"But where did you get all those splendid beasts?" asked Great Claus.

"They are sea-cattle," said Little Claus. "I will tell you the whole story, and indeed I thank you heartily for drowning me. I'm at the top of the tree now and a very rich man, I can tell you. I was so frightened when I was in the sack! The wind whistled in my ears when you threw me over the bridge into the cold water. I immediately sank to the bottom, but I was not hurt, for the grass is beautifully soft down there. The sack was opened at once by a beautiful maiden in snow-white clothes with a green wreath on her wet hair. She took my hand and said, 'Are you there, Little Claus? Here are some cattle for you, and a mile further up the road you will come upon another herd, which I will give you, too!' Then I saw that the river was a great highway for the seafolk. Down at the bottom of it they walked and drove about, from the sea right up to the end of the river. The flowers were lovely and the grass was so fresh; the fishes which swam about glided close to me just like birds in the air. How nice the people were, and what a lot of cattle strolling about in the ditches."

"But why did you come straight up here again then?" asked Great Claus. "I shouldn't have done that, if it was so fine down there."

"Oh," said Little Claus, "that's because I'm wise. You remember I told you that the mermaid said that a mile further up the road—and by the road she means the river, for she can't go anywhere else—I should find another herd of cattle waiting for me. Well, I know how many bends there are in the river, and what a roundabout way it would be. It's ever so much shorter if you can come up on dry land and take the short cuts, you save a couple of miles by it, and get the cattle much sooner."

"Oh, you are a fortunate man!" said Great Claus. "Do you think I could get some sea-cattle if I were to go down to the bottom of the river?"

"I'm sure you would," said Little Claus; "but I can't carry you in the sack to the river; you're too heavy for me. If you like to walk there and then get into the sack, I'll throw you into the river with the greatest pleasure in the world."

"Thank you," said Great Claus; "but if I don't get any sea-cattle when I get down there, see if I don't give you a sound thrashing."

"Oh! don't be so hard on me." They then walked off to the river. As soon as the cattle saw the water, they rushed down to drink. "See what a hurry they're in," said Little Claus; "they want to get down to the bottom again."

"Now, help me," said Great Claus. He then crept into a big sack which had been lying across the back of one of the cows. "Put a big stone in, or I'm afraid I sha'n't sink," said Great Claus.

"Oh, that'll be all right," said Little Claus, but he put a big stone into the sack and gave it a push. Plump went the sack and Great Claus was in the river, where he sank to the bottom at once.

"I'm afraid he won't find any cattle," said Little Claus, as he drove his herd home.

The Swineherd

THERE was once a poor prince; he had only a tiny kingdom, but it was big enough to allow him to marry, and he was bent upon marrying.

Now it certainly was rather bold of him to say to the emperor's daughter, "Will you have me?" He did, however, venture to say so, for his name was known far and wide, and there were hundreds of princesses who would have said, "Yes," and "Thank you, kindly," but see if she would! Just let us hear about it.

A rose tree grew on the grave of the prince's father, it was such a beautiful rose tree; it only bloomed every fifth year, and then only bore one blossom, but what a rose that was! By merely smelling it, one forgot all one's cares and sorrows.

Then he had a nightingale which sang as if every lovely melody in the world dwelt in her little throat. This rose and this nightingale were to be given to the princess, so they were put into great silver caskets and sent to her.

The emperor had them carried before him into the great hall where the princess was playing at "visiting" with her ladies-in-waiting; they had nothing else to do. When she saw the caskets with the gifts she clapped her hands with delight!

"If it were only a little pussy-cat!" said she,—but there was the lovely rose.

44

"Oh, how exquisitely it is made!" said all the ladies-in-waiting.

"It is more than beautiful," said the emperor; "it is neat."

But the princess touched it, and then she was ready to cry.

"Fie, papa!" she said. "It is not made, it is a real one!"

"Fie," said all the ladies-in-waiting. "It is a real one!"

"Well, let us see what there is in the other casket, before we get angry," said the emperor, and out came the nightingale. It sang so beautifully that at first no one could find anything to say against it.

"Superbe! charmant!" said the ladies-in-waiting, for they all had a smattering of French, one spoke it worse than the other.

"How that bird reminds me of our lamented empress's musical box," said an old courtier. "Ah, yes, they are the same tunes, and the same beautiful execution."

"So they are," said the emperor, and he cried like a little child.

"I should hardly think it could be a real one," said the princess.

"Yes, it is a real one," said those who had brought it.

"Oh, let that bird fly away then," said the princess, and she would not hear of allowing the prince to come. But he was not to be crushed. He stained his face brown and black, and, pressing his cap over his eyes, he knocked at the door.

"Good-morning, Emperor," said he. "Can I be taken into service in the palace?"

"Well, there are so many wishing to do that," said the emperor, "but let me see!—yes, I need somebody to look after the pigs, for we have so many of them."

So the prince was made imperial swineherd. A horrid little room was given him near the pigsties, and here he had to live. He sat busily at work all day, and by the evening he had made a beautiful little cooking pot; it had bells all around it and when the pot boiled they tinkled delightfully and played the old tune:

> "Ach du lieber Augustin,
> Alles ist weg, weg, weg!"*

But the greatest charm of all about it was, that, by holding one's finger in the steam, one could immediately smell all the dinners that were being cooked at every stove in the town. Now this was a very different matter from a rose.

The princess came walking along with all her ladies-in-waiting, and when she heard the tune she stopped and looked pleased, for she could play "du lieber Augustin" herself; it was her only tune, and she could only play it with one finger.

"Why, that is my tune," she said. "This must be a cultivated swineherd. Go and ask him what the instrument costs."

So one of the ladies-in-waiting had to go into his room, but she put pattens on first.

"How much do you want for the pot?" she asked.

"I must have ten kisses from the princess," said the swineherd.

"Heaven preserve us!" said the lady.

"I won't take less," said the swineherd.

"Well, what does he say?" asked the princess.

"I really cannot tell you," said the lady-in-waiting, "it is so shocking."

"Then you must whisper it." And she whispered it.

"He is a wretch!" said the princess, and went away at once. But she had only gone a little way when she heard the bells tinkling beautifully:

> "Ach du lieber Augustin."

"Go and ask him if he will take ten kisses from the ladies-in-waiting."

---

*Alas, dear Augustin,
  All is lost, lost, lost!

"No, thank you," said the swineherd—"ten kisses from the princess, or I keep my pot."

"How tiresome it is," said the princess. "Then you will have to stand round me, so that no one may see."

So the ladies-in-waiting stood round her and spread out their skirts while the swineherd took his ten kisses, and then the pot was hers.

What a delight it was to them. The pot was kept on the boil day and night. They knew what was cooking on every stove in the town, from the chamberlain's to the shoemaker's. The ladies-in-waiting danced about and clapped their hands.

"We know who has sweet soup and pancakes for dinner, and who has cutlets! How amusing it is."

"Highly interesting," said the mistress of the robes.

"One must encourage art," she said. "I am the emperor's daughter."

"Heaven preserve us!" they all said.

The swineherd—that is to say, the prince, only nobody knew that he was not a real swineherd—did not let the day pass in idleness, and he now constructed a rattle. When it was swung round it played all the waltzes, galops and jig tunes which have ever been heard since the creation of the world.

"But this is *superbe!*" said the princess, as she walked by. "I have never heard finer compositions. Go and ask him what the instrument costs, but let us have no more kissing."

"He wants a hundred kisses from the princess!" said the lady-in-waiting.

"I think he is mad!" said the princess, and she went away, but she had not gone far when she stopped.

"One must encourage art," she said. "I am the emperor's daughter. Tell him he can have ten kisses, the same as yesterday, and he can take the others from the ladies-in-waiting."

"But we don't like that at all," said the ladies.

"Oh, nonsense! If I can kiss him you can do the same.

Remember that I pay you wages as well as give you board and lodging." So the lady-in-waiting had to go again.

"A hundred kisses from the princess, or let each keep his own."

"Stand in front of me," said she, and all the ladies stood around, while he kissed her.

"Whatever is the meaning of that crowd round the pigsties?" said the emperor, as he stepped out on to the veranda; he rubbed his eyes and put on his spectacles. "Why, it is the ladies-in-waiting, what game are they up to? I must go and see!" So he pulled up the heels of his slippers, for they were shoes which he had trodden down.

Bless us, what a hurry he was in! When he got into the yard, he walked very softly and the ladies were so busy counting the kisses, so that there should be fair play, and neither too few, nor too many kisses, that they never heard the emperor. He stood on tiptoe.

"What is all this?" he said when he saw what was going on, and he hit them on the head with his slipper just as the swineherd was taking his eighty-sixth kiss.

"Out you go!" said the emperor, for he was furious, and both the princess and the prince were put out of his realm.

There she stood crying, and the swineherd scolded, and the rain poured down in torrents.

"Oh, miserable creature that I am! If only I had accepted the handsome prince. Oh, how unhappy I am!"

The swineherd went behind a tree, wiped the black and brown stain from his face, and threw away his ugly clothes. When he stepped out dressed as a prince, he was so handsome that the princess could not help curtseying to him.

"I am come to despise thee," he said. "Thou wouldst not have an honorable prince, thou couldst not prize the rose, or the nightingale, but thou wouldst kiss the swineherd for a trumpery musical box! As thou hast made thy bed, so must thou lie upon it!"

Then he went back into his own little kingdom and shut and locked the door. So she had to stand outside and sing in earnest—

"Ach du lieber Augustin,
Alles ist weg, weg, weg!"

The Ugly Duckling

IN a sunny spot in the country stood an old mansion surrounded by a deep moat. Great dock leaves grew from the walls of the house right down to the water's edge; some of them were so tall that a small child could stand upright under them. In amongst the leaves it was as secluded as in the depths of a forest; and there a duck was sitting on her nest. Her little ducklings were just about to be hatched, but she was nearly tired of sitting; it had lasted such a long time. Moreover, she had very few visitors, as the other ducks liked swimming about in the moat better than waddling up to sit under the dock leaves and gossip with her.

At last one egg after another began to crack. "Cheep, cheep!" they said. All the chicks had come to life, and were poking out their heads.

"Quack! quack!" said the duck; they all quacked their hardest, and looked about them on all sides among the green leaves; their mother allowed them to look as much as they liked, for green is good for the eyes.

"How big the world is, to be sure!" said all the young ones; for they certainly had ever so much more room to move about than when they were inside in the egg shell.

"Do you imagine this is the whole world?" said the mother. "It stretches a long way on the other side of the garden, right into the parson's field; but I have never been as far as that! I suppose you are all here now?" and she got up. "No! I declare I have not got you all yet! The biggest egg is still there; how long is it going to last?" and she settled herself on the nest again.

"Well, how are you getting on?" said an old duck who had come to pay her a visit.

"This one egg is taking such a long time," answered the sitting duck, "the shell will not crack; but now you must look at the others; they are the finest ducklings I have ever seen! they are all exactly like their father, the rascal! he never comes to see me."

"Let me look at the egg that won't crack," said the old duck. "You may be sure that it is a turkey's egg! I have been cheated like that once, and I had no end of trouble and worry with the creatures, for I may tell you that they are afraid of the water. I could not get them into it; I quacked and snapped at them, but it was no good. Let me see the egg! Yes, it is a turkey's egg! You just let it alone and teach the other children to swim."

"I will sit on it a little longer; I have sat so long already, that I may as well go on till the Midsummer Fair comes round."

"Please yourself," said the old duck, and she went away.

At last the big egg cracked. "Cheep, cheep!" said the young one and tumbled out; how big and ugly he was! The duck looked at him.

"That is a monstrous big duckling," she said; "none of the others looked like that; can he be a turkey chick? Well, we shall soon find that out; into the water he shall go, if I have to kick him in myself."

Next day was gloriously fine, and the sun shone on all the green dock leaves. The mother duck with her whole family went down to the moat.

Splash, into the water she sprang. "Quack, quack!" she said, and one duckling plumped in after the other. The water dashed over their heads, but they came up again and floated beautifully; their legs went of themselves, and they were all there; even the big ugly gray one swam about with them.

"No, that is no turkey," she said. "How beautifully he

uses his legs and how erect he holds himself: he is my
own chick! after all, he is not so bad when you come to
look at him properly. Quack, quack! Now come with me
and I will take you into the world, and introduce you to
the duckyard; but keep close to me all the time, so that no
one may tread upon you, and beware of the cat!"

They went into the duckyard. There was a fearful up-
roar going on, for two broods were fighting for the head of
an eel, and in the end the cat captured it.

"That's how things go in this world," said the mother
duck, and she licked her bill, for she wanted the eel's head
herself.

"Use your legs," said she; "mind you quack properly,
and bend your necks to the old duck over there! She is the
grandest of them all; she has Spanish blood in her veins
and that accounts for her size, and, do you see? she has a
red rag round her leg; that is a wonderfully fine thing, and
the most extraordinary mark of distinction any duck can
have. It shows clearly that she is not to be parted with,
and that she is worthy of recognition both by beasts and
men! Quack now! don't turn your toes in; a well brought
up duckling keeps his legs wide apart just like father and
mother; that's it, now bend your necks, and say quack!"

They did as they were bid, but the other ducks round
about looked at them and said, quite loud: "Just look
there! now we are to have that tribe! just as if there were
not enough of us already, and, oh, dear! how ugly that
duckling is; we won't stand him!" and a duck flew at him
at once and bit him in the neck.

"Let him be," said the mother; "he is doing no harm."

"Very likely not, but he is so ungainly and queer," said
the biter; "he must be whacked."

"They are handsome children mother has," said the old
duck with the rag round her leg; "all good looking except
this one. He is not a good specimen; it's a pity you can't
make him over again."

"That can't be done, your grace," said the mother duck;
"he is not handsome, but he is a thorough good creature,

and he swims as beautifully as any of the others; nay, I think I might venture even to add that I think he will improve as he goes on, or perhaps in time he may grow smaller! He was too long in the egg, and so he has not come out with a very good figure." She patted his neck and stroked him down. "Besides he is a drake," said she; "so it does not matter so much. I believe he will be very strong, and I don't doubt but he will make his way in the world."

"The other ducklings are very pretty," said the old duck. "Now make yourselves quite at home, and if you find the head of an eel you may bring it to me!"

After that they felt quite at home. But the poor duckling which had been the last to come out of the shell, and who was so ugly, was bitten, pushed about, and made fun of both by the ducks and the hens. "He is too big," they all said; and the turkey-cock, who was born with his spurs on, and therefore thought himself quite an emperor, puffed himself up like a vessel in full sail, made for him, and gobbled and gobbled till he became quite red in the face. The poor duckling was at his wit's end, and did not know which way to turn; he was in despair because he was so ugly, and the butt of the whole duckyard.

So the first day passed, and afterwards matters grew worse and worse. The poor duckling was chased and hustled by all of them; even his brothers and sisters abused him; and they were always saying, "If only the cat would get hold of you, you hideous object!" Even his mother said, "I wish to goodness you were miles away." The ducks bit him, the hens pecked him, and the girl who fed them kicked him aside.

At last he ran off and flew right over the hedge, where the little birds flew up into the air in a fright.

"That is because I am so ugly," thought the poor duckling, shutting his eyes, but he ran on all the same until he came to a great marsh where the wild ducks lived; he was so tired and miserable that he stayed there the whole night.

In the morning the wild ducks flew up to inspect their new comrade.

"What sort of a creature are you?" they inquired, as the duckling turned from side to side and greeted them as well as he could. "You are frightfully ugly," said the wild ducks, "but that does not matter to us, so long as you do not marry into our family!" Poor fellow! he had not thought of marriage; all he wanted was permission to lie among the rushes, and to drink a little of the marsh water.

He stayed there two whole days, then two wild geese came, or rather two wild ganders; they were not long out of the shell, and therefore rather pert.

"I say, comrade," they said, "you are so ugly that we have taken quite a fancy to you; will you join us and be a bird of passage? There is another marsh close by, and there are some charming wild geese there; all sweet young ladies, who can say quack! You are ugly enough to make your fortune among them." Just at that moment, bang! bang! was heard up above, and both the wild geese fell dead among the reeds, and the water turned blood red. Bang! bang! went the guns, and whole flocks of wild geese flew up from the rushes and the shot peppered among them again.

There was a grand shooting party, and the sportsmen lay hidden round the marsh; some even sat on the branches of the trees which overhung the water; the blue smoke rose like clouds among the dark trees and swept over the pool.

The water-dogs wandered about in the swamp, splash! splash! The rushes and reeds bent beneath their tread on all sides. It was terribly alarming to the poor duckling. He twisted his head round to get it under his wing, and just at that moment a frightful, big dog appeared close beside him; his tongue hung right out of his mouth and his eyes glared wickedly. He opened his great chasm of a mouth close to the duckling, showed his sharp teeth—and—splash—went on without touching him.

"Oh, thank Heaven!" sighed the duckling, "I am so ugly that even the dog won't bite me!"

Then he lay quite still while the shot whistled among the bushes, and bang after bang rent the air. It only became quiet late in the day, but even then the poor duckling did not dare to get up; he waited several hours more before he looked about, and then he hurried away from the marsh as fast as he could. He ran across fields and meadows, and there was such a wind that he had hard work to make his way.

Towards night he reached a poor little cottage; it was such a miserable hovel that it could not make up its mind which way to fall even, and so it remained standing. The wind whistled so fiercely round the duckling that he had to sit on his tail to resist it, and it blew harder and harder; then he saw that the door had fallen off one hinge and hung so crookedly that he could creep into the house through the crack, and by this means he made his way into the room. An old woman lived there with her cat and her hen. The cat, which she called "Sonnie," could arch his back, purr, and give off electric sparks, that is to say if you stroked his fur the wrong way. The hen had quite tiny short legs, and so she was called "Chuckie-low-legs." She laid good eggs, and the old woman was as fond of her as if she had been her own child.

In the morning the strange duckling was immediately discovered and the cat began to purr, and the hen to cluck.

"What on earth is that!" said the old woman, looking round, but her sight was not good, and she thought the duckling was a fat duck which had escaped. "This is a capital find," said she; "now I shall have duck's eggs if only it is not a drake! we must find out about that!"

So she took the duckling on trial for three weeks, but no eggs made their appearance. The cat was the master of the house and the hen the mistress, and they always spoke of "we and the world," for they thought that they represented the half of the world, and that quite the better half.

The duckling thought there might be two opinions on the subject, but the hen would not hear of it.

"Can you lay eggs?" she asked.

"No!"

"Will you have the goodness to hold your tongue then!"

And the cat said, "Can you arch your back, purr, or give off sparks?"

"No."

"Then you had better keep your opinions to yourself when people of sense are speaking!"

The duckling sat in the corner nursing his ill-humor; then he began to think of the fresh air and the sunshine, an uncontrollable longing seized him to float on the water, and at last he could not help telling the hen about it.

"What on earth possesses you?" she asked; "you have nothing to do, that is why you get these freaks into your head. Lay some eggs or take to purring, and you will get over it."

"But it is so delicious to float on the water," said the duckling; "so delicious to feel it rushing over your head when you dive to the bottom."

"That would be a fine amusement," said the hen. "I think you have gone mad. Ask the cat about it; he is the wisest creature I know; ask him if he is fond of floating on the water or diving under it. I say nothing about myself. Ask our mistress, the old woman; there is no one in the world cleverer than she is. Do you suppose she has any desire to float on the water, or to duck underneath it?"

"You do not understand me," said the duckling.

"Well, if we don't understand you, who should? I suppose you don't consider yourself cleverer than the cat or the old woman, not to mention me. Don't make a fool of yourself, child, and thank your stars for all the good we have done you! Have you not lived in this warm room, and in such society that you might have learned something? But you are an idiot, and there is no pleasure in associating with you. You may believe me I mean you well, I tell you home truths, and there is no surer way than that of knowing who are one's friends. You just see about laying some eggs, or learn to purr, or to emit sparks."

"I think I will go out into the wide world," said the duckling.

"Oh, do so by all means," said the hen.

So away went the duckling; he floated on the water and ducked underneath it, but he was looked askance at by every living creature for his ugliness. Now the autumn came on; the leaves in the woods turned yellow and brown; the wind took hold of them, and they danced about. The sky looked very cold, and the clouds hung heavy with snow and hail. A raven stood on the fence and croaked caw! caw! from sheer cold; it made one shiver only to think of it; the poor duckling certainly was in a bad case.

One evening, the sun was just setting in wintry splendor, when a flock of beautiful large birds appeared out of the bushes; the duckling had never seen anything so beautiful. They were dazzlingly white with long waving necks; they were swans, and uttering a peculiar cry, they spread out their magnificent broad wings and flew away from the cold regions to warmer lands and open seas. They mounted so high, so very high! The ugly little duckling became strangely uneasy; he circled round and round in the water like a wheel, craning his neck up into the air after them. Then he uttered a shriek so piercing and so strange, that he quite frightened himself. Oh, he could not forget those beautiful birds, those happy birds, and as soon as they were out of sight he ducked right down to the bottom, and when he came up again he was quite beside himself. He did not know what the birds were, or whither they flew, but all the same he was more drawn towards them than he had ever been by any creatures before. He did not envy them in the least; how could it occur to him even to wish to be such a marvel of beauty? He would have been thankful if only the ducks would have tolerated him among them—the poor ugly creature!

The winter was so bitterly cold that the duckling was obliged to swim about in the water to keep it from freezing, but every night the hole in which he swam got smaller and smaller. Then it froze so hard that the surface ice cracked, and the duckling had to use his legs all the time, so that the ice should not close in round him; at last he was so weary that he could move no more, and he was frozen fast into the ice.

Early in the morning a peasant came along and saw him; he went out onto the ice and hammered a hole in it with his heavy wooden shoe, and carried the duckling home to his wife. There it soon revived. The children wanted to play with it, but the duckling thought they were going to abuse him, and rushed in his fright into the milk pan, and the milk spurted out all over the room. The woman shrieked and threw up her hands. The duckling flew into the butter cask, and down into the meal tub and out again. Just imagine what it looked like by this time! The woman screamed and tried to hit it with the tongs, and the children tumbled over one another in trying to catch it, and they screamed with laughter—by good luck the door stood open, and the duckling flew out among the bushes and the new fallen snow—and it lay there thoroughly exhausted.

But it would be too sad to mention all the privation and misery it had to go through during that hard winter. When the sun began to shine warmly again, the duckling was in the marsh, lying among the rushes; the larks were singing and the beautiful spring had come.

When all at once it raised its wings, they flapped with much greater strength than before, and bore him off vigorously. Before he knew where he was, he found himself in a large garden where the apple trees were in full blossom, and the air was scented with lilacs; the long branches overhung the indented shores of the lake! Oh! the spring freshness was so delicious!

Just in front of him he saw three beautiful white swans advancing towards him from a thicket; with rustling feathers they swam lightly over the water. The duckling recognized the majestic birds, and he was overcome by a strange melancholy.

"I will fly to them, the royal birds, and they will hack me to pieces, because I, who am so ugly, venture to approach them! But it won't matter; better be killed by them than be snapped at by the ducks, pecked by the hens, or spurned by the henwife, or suffer so much misery in the winter."

So he flew into the water and swam towards the stately swans; they saw him and darted towards him with ruffled feathers.

"Kill me, oh, kill me!" said the poor creature, and bowing his head towards the water he awaited his death. But what did he see reflected in the transparent water?

He saw below him his own image, but he was no longer a clumsy dark gray bird, ugly and ungainly; he was himself a swan! It does not matter in the least having been born in a duckyard, if only you come out of a swan's egg!

He felt quite glad of all the misery and tribulation he had gone through; he was the better able to appreciate his good fortune now, and all the beauty which greeted him. The big swans swam round and round him, and stroked him with their bills.

Some little children came into the garden with corn and pieces of bread, which they threw into the water; and the smallest one cried out, "There is a new one!" The other children shouted with joy, "Yes, a new one has come!" And they clapped their hands and danced about, running after their father and mother. They threw the bread into the water, and one and all said: "The new one is the prettiest! He is so young and handsome." And the old swans bent their heads and did homage before him.

He felt quite shy, and hid his head under his wing; he did not know what to think; he was so happy, but not at all proud; a good heart never becomes proud. He thought of how he had been pursued and scorned, and now he heard them all say that he was the most beautiful of all beautiful birds. The lilacs bent their boughs right down into the water before him, and the bright sun was warm and cheering, and he rustled his feathers and raised his slender neck aloft, saying with exultation in his heart: "I never dreamed of so much happiness when I was the Ugly Duckling!"

The Emperor's New Clothes

MANY years ago there was an emperor who was so very fond of new clothes that he spent all his money on them. He cared nothing about his soldiers nor about the theater, nor for driving in the woods except for the sake of showing off his new clothes. He had a costume for every hour in the day, and instead of saying as one does about any other king or emperor, "He is in his council chamber," they always said, "The emperor is in his dressing-room."

Life was very gay in the great town where he lived; hosts of strangers came to visit it every day. Among the visitors one day came two swindlers. They gave themselves out as weavers, and said that they knew how to weave the most beautiful stuffs imaginable. Not only were the colors and patterns unusually fine, but the clothes that were made of the cloth had the peculiar quality of becoming invisible to anyone who was not fit for the office he held, or who was impossibly dull.

"Those must be splendid clothes," thought the emperor. "By wearing them I should be able to discover which men in my kingdom are unfitted for their posts. I shall distinguish the wise men from the fools. Yes, I certainly must order some of that stuff to be woven for me."

He paid the two swindlers a lot of money in advance, so that they might begin their work at once.

They did put up two looms and pretended to weave, but they had nothing whatever upon their shuttles. At the outset they asked for a quantity of the finest silk and the purest gold thread, all of which they put into their own bags while they worked away at the empty looms far into the night.

"I should like to know how those weavers are getting on with the stuff," thought the emperor; but he felt a little queer when he reflected that anyone who was stupid or unfit for his post would not be able to see it. He certainly thought that he need have no fears for himself, but still he thought he would send somebody else first to see how it was getting on. Everybody in the town knew what wonderful power the cloth possessed, and everyone was anxious to see how stupid his neighbor was.

"I will send my faithful old minister to the weavers," thought the emperor. "He will be best able to see how the stuff looks, for he is a clever man and no one fulfills his duties better than he does!"

So the good old minister went into the room where the two swindlers sat working at the empty loom.

"Heaven preserve us!" thought the old minister, opening his eyes very wide. "Why I can't see a thing!" But he took care not to say so.

Both the swindlers begged him to be good enough to step a little nearer, and asked if he did not think it a good pattern and beautiful coloring. They pointed to the empty loom, and the poor old minister stared as hard as he could, but he could not see anything, for of course there was nothing to see.

"Good heavens!" thought he, "is it possible that I am a fool? I have never thought so, and nobody must know it. Am I not fit for my post? It will never do to say that I cannot see the cloths."

"Well, sir, you don't say anything about the stuff," said the one who was pretending to weave.

"Oh, it is beautiful! quite charming!" said the minister looking through his spectacles; "this pattern and these colors! I will certainly tell the emperor that the stuff pleases me very much."

"We are delighted to hear you say so," said the swindlers, and then they named all the colors and described the peculiar pattern. The old minister paid great attention to what they said, so as to be able to repeat it when he got home to the emperor.

Then the swindlers went on to demand more money, more silk, and more gold, to be able to proceed with the weaving, and they put it all into their own pockets—not a single strand was ever put into the loom, but they went on as before weaving at the empty loom.

The emperor soon sent another faithful official to see how the stuff was getting on, and if it would soon be ready. The same thing happened to him as to the minister; he looked and looked, but as there was only the empty loom, he could see nothing at all.

"Is not this a beautiful piece of stuff?" said both the swindlers, showing and explaining the beautiful pattern and colors which were not there to be seen.

"I know I am no fool!" thought the man, "so it must be that I am unfit for my good post! It is very strange though! however one must not let it appear!" So he praised the stuff he did not see, and assured them of his delight in the beautiful colors and the originality of the design. "It is absolutely charming!" he said to the emperor. Everybody in the town was talking about this splendid stuff.

Now the emperor thought he would like to see it while it was still on the loom. So, accompanied by a number of selected courtiers, among whom were the two faithful officials who had already seen the imaginary stuff, he went to visit the crafty impostors, who were working away as hard as ever they could at the empty loom.

"It is magnificent!" said both the honest officials. "Only see, your Majesty, what a design! What colors!" And they pointed to the empty loom, for they thought no doubt the others could see the stuff.

"What!" thought the emperor; "I see nothing at all! This is terrible! Am I a fool? Am I not fit to be emperor? Why, nothing worse could happen to me!"

"Oh, it is beautiful!" said the emperor. "It has my highest approval!" and he nodded his satisfaction as he gazed at the empty loom. Nothing would make him say that he could not see anything.

The whole suite gazed and gazed, but saw nothing more than all the others. However, they all exclaimed with his Majesty, "It is very beautiful!" and they advised him to wear a suit made of this wonderful cloth on the occasion of a great procession which was just about to take place.

"It is magnificent! gorgeous! excellent!" went from mouth to mouth. They were all equally delighted with it. The emperor gave each of the rogues an order of knighthood to be worn in their buttonholes and the title of "Gentlemen weavers."

The swindlers sat up the whole night, before the day on which the procession was to take place, burning sixteen candles; so that people might see how anxious they were to get the emperor's new clothes ready. They pretended to take the stuff off the loom. They cut it out in the air with a huge pair of scissors, and they stitched away with needles without any thread in them. At last they said: "Now the emperor's new clothes are ready!"

The emperor, with his grandest courtiers, went to them himself, and both swindlers raised one arm in the air, as if they were holding something, and said: "See, these are the trousers, this is the coat, here is the mantle!" and so on. "It is as light as a spider's web. One might think one had nothing on, but that is the very beauty of it!"

"Yes!" said all the courtiers, but they could not see anything, for there was nothing to see.

"Will your Imperial Majesty be graciously pleased to take off your clothes," said the impostors, "so that we may put on the new ones, along here before the great mirror."

The emperor took off all his clothes, and the impostors pretended to give him one article of dress after the other, of the new ones which they had pretended to make. They pretended to fasten something round his waist and to tie on the train, and the emperor turned round and round in front of the mirror.

"How well his Majesty looks in the new clothes! How becoming they are!" cried all the people around him. "What a design, and what colors! They are most gorgeous robes!"

"The canopy is waiting outside which is to be carried over your Majesty in the procession," said the master of the ceremonies.

"Well, I am quite ready," said the emperor. "Don't the clothes fit well?" and then he turned round again in front of the mirror, so that he should seem to be looking at his grand things.

The chamberlains who were to carry the train stopped and pretended to lift it from the ground with both hands, and they walked along with their hands in the air. They dared not let it appear that they could not see anything.

Then the emperor walked along in the procession under the gorgeous canopy, and everybody in the streets and at the windows exclaimed, "How beautiful the emperor's new clothes are! What a splendid train! And they fit to perfection!" Nobody would let it appear that he could see nothing, for then he would be proved unfit for his post, or else a fool.

None of the emperor's clothes had been so successful before.

"But he has got nothing on," said a little child.

"Oh, listen to the innocent," said its father. Then one person whispered to the other what the child had said. "He has nothing on! A child says he has nothing on!"

"But he has nothing on!" at last cried all the people.

The emperor writhed, for he knew it was true, but he thought "the procession must go on now," so he held himself stiffer than ever, and the chamberlains held up the invisible train.

The Princess on the Pea

THERE was once a prince, and he wanted to marry a princess, but she must be a real princess. He traveled right round the world to find one, but there was always something wrong. There were plenty of princesses, but whether they were real princesses he couldn't make sure for there was always something not quite right about them. So at last he had to come home again, and he was very sad because he wanted a real princess so badly.

One evening there was a terrible storm; with thunder and lightning and the rain pouring down in torrents; it was a fearful night.

In the middle of the storm somebody knocked at the town gate, and the old king himself went to open it.

It was a princess who stood outside, but she was in a terrible state from the rain and the storm. The water streamed out of her hair and her clothes, it ran in at the top of her shoes and out at the heel, but she said that she was a real princess.

"Well we shall soon see if that is true," thought the old queen, but she did not say so. She went into the bedroom where the princess was to sleep and took all the bedclothes off, then she laid a pea on the bedstead and took twenty mattresses and piled them on the top of the pea, and then twenty feather beds on the top of the mattresses. In the morning they asked the princess how she had slept.

"Oh terribly badly!" said the princess. "I have hardly

closed my eyes the whole night! Heaven knows what was in the bed. I seemed to be lying upon some hard thing, and my whole body is black and blue this morning. It is terrible!"

They at once saw that she must be a real princess since she had felt the pea through twenty mattresses and twenty feather beds. Nobody but a real princess could have such a delicate skin.

So the prince took her to be his wife, for now he was sure that he had found a real princess, and the pea was put into a Museum, where it may still be seen if no one has stolen it.

Now this is a true story.

The Red Shoes

THERE was once a tiny, delicate little girl, who was so poor that she always had to go about barefoot in summer. In winter she only had a pair of heavy wooden shoes, which chafed her ankles terribly.

An old mother shoemaker, who lived in the middle of the village, made a pair of little shoes out of some strips of red cloth. They were very clumsy, but she made them out of pity for the little girl whose name was Karen.

These shoes were given to her, and she wore them for the first time on the day her mother was buried; they were certainly not mourning, but she had no others, and so she walked barelegged in them behind the poor pine coffin.

A big old carriage happened to drive by, and a big old lady was seated in it; she looked at the little girl, and felt very, very sorry for her, and said to the parson, "Give the little girl to me and I will look after her and be kind to her." Karen thought it was all because of the red shoes, but the old lady said they were hideous, and had them burned. Karen was well and neatly dressed. She had to learn reading and sewing. People said she was pretty, but her mirror said, "You are more than pretty, you are lovely."

One day the queen passed through that part of the country; she had her little daughter the princess with her. Karen, with many other people, crowded round the palace where they were staying, to see them. The little princess appeared at a window. She wore neither a train nor a golden crown, but she was dressed all in white with a beautiful pair of red morocco shoes. They were not at all like those the poor old mother shoemaker had made for Karen. She had never seen anything as beautiful as these red shoes.

The time came when Karen was old enough to be confirmed; she had new clothes, and she was to have a pair of new shoes. The rich shoemaker in the town was to take the measure of her little foot; his shop was full of glass cases of the loveliest shoes and boots. They looked tempting, but the old lady could not see very well, so it gave her no pleasure to look at them. Among all the other shoes there was one pair of red shoes like those worn by the princess. Oh, how pretty they were! The shoemaker told them that they had been made for an earl's daughter, but they had not fitted. "I suppose they are patent leather," said the old lady, "they are so shiny."

"Yes, indeed, they do shine," said Karen, and she tried them on. They fitted and were bought; but the old lady had not the least idea that they were red. She would never have allowed Karen to wear red shoes for her Confirmation.

Everybody looked at Karen's feet when she walked up the church to the chancel; even the old pictures, those portraits of old priests and their wives, with stiff collars and long black clothes, seemed to fix their eyes upon her shoes. She thought of nothing else when the minister laid his hand upon her head and spoke to her of holy baptism, the covenant of God, and told her that from henceforth she was to be a responsible Christian person. The solemn notes of the organ resounded, the children sang with their sweet voices, the old precentor sang, but Karen thought of nothing but her red shoes.

By the afternoon several persons had told the old lady that the shoes were red, and she told Karen that it was very naughty and most improper. For the future, whenever Karen went to the church she was to wear black shoes, even if they were old. Next Sunday there was Holy Communion. Karen looked at the black shoes and then at the red ones—then she looked again at the red, and at last put them on.

It was beautiful, sunny weather; Karen and the old lady went by the path through the corn-field, which was rather dusty. By the church door stood a lame old soldier. He carried a crutch and he had a curious long beard, it was more red than white, in fact it was almost quite red. He bent down to the ground and asked the old lady if he might dust her shoes. Karen put out her little foot, too. "What beautiful dancing shoes!" said the soldier. "Mind you stick fast when you dance," and as he spoke he struck the soles with his hand. The old lady gave the soldier a copper and went into the church with Karen. All the people in the church looked at Karen's red shoes, and all the portraits looked, too. When Karen knelt at the altar-rails and the chalice was put to her lips, she only thought of the red shoes; she seemed to see them floating before her eyes. She forgot to join in the hymn of praise, and she forgot to say the Lord's Prayer.

When everybody left the church, and the old lady got into her carriage, Karen lifted her foot to get in after her, but the old soldier, who was still standing there, said, "See what pretty dancing shoes!"

Karen couldn't help it; she took a few dancing steps. But when she had begun, her feet kept on dancing. The shoes seemed to have a power over them. She danced right round the church and couldn't stop; the coachman had to run after her and take hold of her, and lift her into the carriage; but her feet continued to dance, so that she kicked the poor lady horribly. At last they got the shoes off, and her feet had a little rest.

When they got home the shoes were put away in a cupboard, but Karen could not help going to look at them.

The old lady became very ill; she had to be carefully nursed and tended, and no one was nearer than Karen to do this. But there was to be a grand ball in the town, and Karen was invited. She looked at the old lady, and she looked at the red shoes. She thought there was no harm in doing so and she even put on the red shoes; but then she went to the ball and began to dance!

The shoes would not let her do what she liked: when she wanted to go to the right, they danced to the left: when she wanted to dance up the room, the shoes danced down the room. They danced down the stairs, through the streets and out of the town gate. Away she danced, and away she had to dance, right away into the dark forest. Something shone up above the trees, and she thought it was the moon. But it was the face of the old soldier with the red beard, and he nodded and said, "See what pretty dancing shoes!"

This frightened her terribly and she tried to throw off the red shoes, but they stuck fast. She tore off her stockings, but the shoes had grown fast to her feet, and off she danced, and off she had to dance over fields and meadows, in rain and sunshine, by day and by night, but at night it was fearful.

She danced into the open churchyard, and she tried to sit down on a pauper's grave where the bitter wormwood grew, but there was no rest nor repose for her. When she danced towards the open church door, she saw an angel standing there in long white robes; his wings reached from his shoulders to the ground, his face was grave and stern, and in his hand he held a broad and shining sword.

"Dance and dance," said he, "you shall dance in your red shoes till you are pale and cold. You shall dance from door to door, and wherever you find proud vain children, you must knock at the door so that they may see you and fear you."

"Mercy!" shrieked Karen, but she did not hear the angel's answer, for the shoes bore her through the gate into the fields over roadways and paths, ever and ever she was forced to dance.

One morning she danced past a door she knew well; she heard the sound of a hymn from within, and she knew that the old lady was dead, and it seemed to her that she was forsaken by all the world.

On and on she danced; the shoes bore her over briars and stubble till her feet were torn and bleeding. She danced over the heath till she came to a little lonely house. She knew the executioner lived here, and she tapped with her fingers on the window pane and said,—

"Come out! come out! I can't come in for I am dancing!"

The executioner said, "You can't know who I am! I chop the bad people's heads off, and I see that my ax is quivering."

"Don't chop my head off," said Karen, "for then I can never repent of my sins, but pray, pray chop off my feet with the red shoes!"

Then she confessed all her sins, and the executioner chopped off her feet with the red shoes, and they danced away with the little feet into the depths of the forest.

Then he made her a pair of wooden feet and crutches, and he taught her the psalm, that penitents sing; and she kissed the hand which had wielded the ax, and went away over the heath.

"I have suffered enough for those red shoes!" said she. "I will go to church now, so that they may see me!" and she went as fast as she could to the church door. When she got there, the red shoes danced right up in front of her. She was so frightened that she went home again.

She was very sad all the week, and shed many bitter tears, but when Sunday came, she said, "Now then, I have suffered and struggled long enough; I should think I am quite as good as many who sit holding their heads so high in church!" She went along quite boldly, but she did not get further than the gate before she saw the red shoes dancing in front of her; she was more frightened than ever, and turned back, this time with real repentance in her heart. Then she went to the parson's house, and begged to be taken into service, she would be very industrious and work as hard as she could, she didn't care what wages they gave her, if only she might have a roof over her head and live among kind people. The parson's wife was sorry for her, and took her into her service. Karen became very industrious and thoughtful. She would sit and listen most attentively in the evening when the parson read the Bible. All the little ones were very fond of her, but when they chattered about finery and dress, and about being as beautiful as a queen, she would shake her head.

On Sunday they all went to church. When they asked her if she would go with them she looked sadly, with tears in her eyes, at her crutches, and they went without her to hear the word of God, while she sat in her little room alone. It was only big enough for a bed and a chair; she sat there with her prayer-book in her hand, and as she read it with a humble mind, she heard the notes of the organ, borne from the church by the wind, and she raised her tear-stained face and said, "Oh, God help me!"

Then the sun shone brightly round her, and the angel in the white robes whom she had seen on yonder night, at the church door, stood before her. He no longer held the sharp sword in his hand, but a beautiful green branch, covered with roses. He touched the ceiling with it and it rose to a great height, and wherever he touched it a golden star appeared. Then he touched the walls and they spread themselves out, and she saw and heard the organ. She saw the pictures of the old parsons and their wives; the congregation were all sitting in their seats singing aloud—for the church itself had come home to the poor girl, in her narrow little chamber, or else she had been taken to it. She found herself on the bench with the other people from the Parsonage. And when the hymn had come to an end they looked up and said, "It was fine that you came after all, little Karen!"

"It was through God's mercy!" she said. The organ sounded, and the children's voices echoed sweetly through the choir. The warm sunshine streamed brightly in through the window, right up to the bench where Karen sat; her heart was so overfilled with the sunshine, with peace, and with joy, that it broke. Her soul flew with the sunshine to heaven, and no one there ever asked about the red shoes.

The Steadfast Tin Soldier

THERE were once five and twenty tin soldiers, all brothers, for they were the offspring of the same old tin
spoon. Each man shouldered his gun, kept his eyes well to
the front, and wore the smartest red and blue uniform
imaginable. The first thing they heard in their new world,
when the lid was taken off the box, was a little boy clapping his hands and crying, "Soldiers, soldiers!" It was his
birthday and they had just been given to him; so he lost
no time in setting them up on the table. All the soldiers
were exactly alike with one exception, and he differed
from the rest in having only one leg. For he was made last,
and there was not quite enough tin left to finish him. However, he stood just as well on his one leg, as the others on
two, in fact he is the very one who is to become famous.
On the table where they were being set up, were many
other toys; but the chief thing which caught the eye was
a delightful paper castle. You could see through the tiny
windows, right into the rooms. Outside there were some
little trees surrounding a small mirror, representing a lake,
whose surface reflected the waxen swans which were
swimming about on it. It was altogether charming, but the
prettiest thing of all was a little maiden standing at the
open door of the castle. She, too, was cut out of paper, but
she wore a dress of the lightest gauze, with a dainty little
blue ribbon over her shoulders, by way of a scarf, set off
by a brilliant spangle, as big as her whole face. The little
maid was stretching out both arms, for she was a dancer,

and in the dance, one of her legs was raised so high into the air that the tin soldier could see absolutely nothing of it, and supposed that she, like himself, had but one leg.

"That would be the very wife for me!" he thought; "but she is much too grand; she lives in a palace, while I only have a box, and then there are five and twenty of us to share it. No, that would be no place for her, but I must try to make her acquaintance!" Then he lay down full length behind a snuff box, which stood on the table. From that point he could have a good look at the little lady, who continued to stand on one leg without losing her balance.

Late in the evening the other soldiers were put into their box, and the people of the house went to bed. Now was the time for the toys to play; they amused themselves with paying visits, fighting battles, and giving balls. The tin soldiers rustled about in their box, for they wanted to join the games, but they could not get the lid off. The nutcrackers turned somersaults, and the pencil scribbled nonsense on the slate. There was such a noise that the canary woke up and joined in, but his remarks were in verse. The only two who did not move were the tin soldier and the little dancer. She stood as stiff as ever on tiptoe, with her arms spread out; he was equally firm on his one leg, and he did not take his eyes off her for a moment.

Then the clock struck twelve, and pop! up flew the lid of the snuff box, but there was no snuff in it, no! There was a little black goblin, a sort of Jack-in-the-box.

"Tin soldier!" said the goblin, "have the goodness to keep your eyes to yourself."

But the tin soldier feigned not to hear.

"Ah! you just wait till to-morrow," said the goblin.

In the morning, when the children got up, they put the tin soldier on the window frame, and, whether it was caused by the goblin or by a puff of wind, I do not know, but all at once the window burst open, and the soldier fell head foremost from the third story.

It was a terrific descent, and he landed at last, with his leg in the air, and rested on his cap, with his bayonet fixed between two paving stones. The maid-servant and the little boy ran down at once to look for him, but although they almost trod on him, they could not see him. Had the soldier only called out, "Here I am," they would easily have found him, but he did not think it proper to shout when he was in uniform.

Presently it began to rain, and the drops fell faster and faster, till there was a regular torrent. When it was over two street boys came along.

"Look out!" said one; "there is a tin soldier! He shall go for a sail!"

So they made a boat out of a newspaper and put the soldier into the middle of it, and he sailed away down the gutter; both boys ran alongside clapping their hands. Good heavens! what waves there were in the gutter, and what a current, but then it certainly had rained cats and dogs. The paper boat danced up and down, and now and then whirled round and round. A shudder ran through the tin soldier, but he remained undaunted, and did not move a muscle, only looked straight before him with his gun shouldered. All at once the boat drifted under a long wooden tunnel, and it became as dark as it was in his box.

"Where am I going now!" thought he. "Well, well, it is all the fault of that goblin! Oh, if only the little maiden were with me in the boat it might be twice as dark for all I should care!"

At this moment a big water rat, who lived in the tunnel, came up.

"Have you a pass?" asked the rat. "Hand up your pass!"

The tin soldier did not speak, but clung still tighter to his gun. The boat rushed on, the rat close behind. Phew, how he gnashed his teeth and shouted to the bits of stick and straw.

"Stop him, stop him, he hasn't paid his toll! He hasn't shown his pass!"

But the current grew stronger and stronger, the tin soldier could already see daylight before him at the end of the tunnel; but he also heard a roaring sound, fit to strike terror to the bravest heart. Just imagine! Where the tunnel ended the stream rushed straight into the big canal. That would be just as dangerous for him as it would be for us to shoot a great rapid.

He was so near the end now that it was impossible to stop. The boat dashed out; the poor tin soldier held himself as stiff as he could; no one should say of him that he even winced.

The boat swirled round three or four times, and filled with water to the edge; it must sink. The tin soldier stood up to his neck in water, and the boat sank deeper and deeper. The paper became limper and limper, and at last the water went over his head—then he thought of the pretty little dancer, whom he was never to see again, and this refrain rang in his ears:

> "Onward! Onward! Soldier!
> For death thou canst not shun."

At last the paper gave way entirely and the soldier fell through—but at that moment he was swallowed by a big fish.

Oh! how dark it was inside the fish, it was worse than being in the tunnel even, and it was so narrow! But the tin soldier was as dauntless as ever, and lay full length shouldering his gun.

The fish rushed about and made the most frantic movements. At last it became quite quiet, and after a time, a flash like lightning pierced it. The soldier was once more in the broad daylight, and someone called out loudly, "A tin soldier!" The fish had been caught, taken to market, sold, and brought into the kitchen, where the cook cut it open with a large knife. She took the soldier up by the waist, with two fingers, and carried him into the parlor, where everyone wanted to see the wonderful man, who had traveled about in the stomach of a fish; but the tin soldier was not at all proud. They set him up on the table, and, wonder of wonders! he found himself in the very same room that he had been in before. He saw the very same children, and the toys were still standing on the table, as well as the beautiful castle with the pretty little dancer.

She still stood on one leg, and held the other up in the air. You see she also was unbending. The soldier was so much moved that he was ready to shed tears of tin, but that would not have been fitting. He looked at her, and she looked at him, but they said never a word. At this moment one of the little boys took up the tin soldier, and without rhyme or reason, threw him into the fire. No doubt the little goblin in the snuff box was to blame for that. The tin soldier stood there, lighted up by the flame, and in the most horrible heat; but whether it was the heat of the real fire, or the warmth of his feelings, he did not know. He had lost all his gay color; it might have been from his perilous journey, or it might have been from grief, who can tell?

He looked at the little maiden, and she looked at him, and he felt that he was melting away, but he still managed to keep himself erect, shouldering his gun bravely.

A door was suddenly opened, and draught caught the little dancer and she fluttered like a sylph, straight into the fire, to the soldier. When the maid took away the ashes next morning she found in them a small tin heart. But of the dancer nothing remained but the spangle, and that was burned as black as a coal.

Thumbelina

THERE was once a woman who wished very much to have a little child, and at last she went to a fairy, and said, "I should so very much like to have a little child; can you tell me where I can find one?"

"Oh, that can be easily managed," said the fairy. "Here is a grain of barley different from the kind that grows in the fields and feeds the chickens; plant it in a flower pot and see what will happen."

"Thank you," said the woman, and she gave the fairy twelve pennies, then she went home and planted the barley corn, and immediately there grew up a large handsome flower, something like a tulip, but with its leaves tightly closed as if it were still a bud. "It is a beautiful flower," said the woman, and she kissed the red and golden-colored leaves. While she kissed the flower it opened, and she could see that it was a real tulip. Within the flower, upon the green velvet stamens, sat a very delicate and graceful little maiden. She was scarcely half as long as a thumb, so she was named "Thumbelina," because she was so small. A walnut-shell, elegantly polished, served her for a cradle; her mattress was made of blue violet-leaves, with a rose-leaf for a counter-pane. Here she slept at night, but during the day she amused herself on a table, where the woman had placed a plate full of water. Round this plate were flowers with their stems in the water, and upon it floated a large tulip-petal, which served Thumbelina for a boat. Here the little girl sat and rowed herself from side to side, with two oars made of white horsehair. It really was a very pretty sight. Thumbelina could sing so softly and sweetly that nothing so sweet had ever before been heard.

One night, while she lay in her pretty bed, a large, ugly, wet toad crept through a broken pane of glass in the window, and leaped right upon the table where Thumbelina lay sleeping under her rose-leaf quilt. "What a pretty little wife this would make for my son!" said the toad, and she took up the walnut-shell in which little Thumbelina lay asleep, and jumped through the window with it into the garden.

In the swampy margin of a broad stream in the garden lived the toad, with her son. He was uglier even than his mother, and when he saw the pretty little maiden in her elegant bed, he could only cry, "Coax, Coax, Buk-ke-kex."

"Don't speak so loud, or she will awake," said the toad, "and then she might run away, for she is as light as swan's down. We will place her on one of the water-lily leaves out in the stream; it will be like an island to her, she is so light and small, and then she cannot escape; and, while she is away, we will make haste and prepare the state-room under the marsh, in which you are to live when you are married."

Far out in the stream grew a number of water-lilies, with broad green leaves, which seemed to float on the top of the water. The largest of these leaves appeared farther off than the rest, and the old toad swam out to it with the walnut-shell, in which little Thumbelina lay still asleep.

The little girl woke very early in the morning, and began to cry bitterly when she found where she was, for she could see nothing but water on every side of the large green leaf, and no way of reaching the land. Meanwhile the old toad was very busy under the marsh, decking her room with rushes and yellow wild flowers, to make it look pretty for her new daughter-in-law. Then she swam out with her ugly son to the leaf on which she had placed poor little Thumbelina. She wanted to fetch the pretty bed, to put it in the bridal chamber for her.

The old toad bowed low to her in the water, and said, "Here is my son; he will be your husband, and you will live happily together in the marsh by the stream."

"Coax, Coax, Buk-ke-kex," was all her son could say for himself; so the toad took up the elegant little bed, and swam away with it, leaving Thumbelina all alone on the green leaf, where she sat and wept. She could not bear to think of living with the old toad, and having her ugly son for a husband. The little fishes, who swam about in the water beneath, had seen the toad, and had heard what she said, so they lifted their heads above the water to look at the little maiden. They saw that she was very pretty, and it made them sorry to think that she must go and live with the ugly toads. "No, we must not allow that!" So they assembled in the water, round the green stalk which held the leaf on which the little maiden stood, and gnawed it away at the root with their teeth. Then the leaf floated down the stream, carrying Thumbelina far away, out of reach of land.

Thumbelina sailed past many towns, and the little birds in the bushes saw her, and sang, "What a lovely little creature!" so the leaf swam away with her farther and farther, till it brought her to other lands. A graceful white butterfly constantly fluttered round her, and at last alighted on the leaf. Thumbelina pleased him, and she was glad of it, for now the toad could not possibly reach her, and the country through which she sailed was beautiful, and the sun shone upon the water, till it glittered like liquid gold. She took off her girdle and tied one end of it round the butterfly, and the other end of the ribbon she fastened to the leaf, which now glided on much faster than ever, taking little Thumbelina with it as she stood. Presently a large June-bug flew by; the moment he caught sight of her, he seized her round her delicate waist with his claws, and flew with her into a tree. The green leaf floated away on the brook, and the butterfly flew with it, for he was fastened to it, and could not get away.

Oh, how frightened little Thumbelina felt when the June-bug flew with her to the tree! The beautiful white butterfly floated away with the leaf, but the June-bug did not trouble himself at all about that. He seated himself by her side on a large green leaf, gave her some honey from the flowers to eat, and told her she was very pretty, though not in the least like a June-bug. After a time, all the June-bugs who lived in the tree came to visit her. They stared at Thumbelina, and then the young lady June-bugs turned up their feelers, and said, "She has only two legs! how ugly that looks." "She has no feelers," said another. "Her waist is quite slim. Pooh! she is like a human being."

"Oh! she is ugly," said all the lady June-bugs, although Thumbelina was very pretty. Then the June-bug who had run away with her believed all the others when they said she was ugly, and would have nothing more to say to her, and told her she might go where she liked. He flew down with her from the tree, and placed her on a daisy, where she cried because she was so ugly that even the June-bugs would have nothing to do with her. And yet she was really the loveliest creature that one could imagine, and as tender and delicate as a beautiful rose-leaf. Poor little Thumbelina lived quite alone in the wide forest all that summer. She wove herself a bed with blades of grass, and hung it up under a broad leaf, to protect herself from the rain. She sucked the honey from the flowers for food, and drank the dew from their leaves every morning. So the summer and the autumn passed away, and then came the winter—the long, cold winter. All the birds who had sung to her so sweetly flew away, and the trees and the flowers were withered. The large clover leaf, under which she had lived, had shriveled up, and left nothing but a dry yellow stalk. She shivered with cold, for her clothes were worn out. It began to snow and each flake was like a whole shovelful falling upon one of us, for we are large, but she was only an inch high. Then she wrapped herself up in a

dry leaf, but that cracked in the middle, and did not keep
her warm, and she shook with cold.

Near the wood in which she had been living lay a large
corn-field, but the corn had been cut a long time, and
nothing remained but the bare, dry stubble standing up
out of the frozen ground. It was like a large wood to her.
Oh! how she shivered with the cold. She came at last to
the door of a field-mouse, who had a little home under the
corn-stubble. The field-mouse lived there, warm and comfortable, with a whole roomful of corn, a kitchen, and a
beautiful dining-room. Poor little Thumbelina stood before the door like a little beggar-girl, and begged for a
small piece of barleycorn, for she had been without a
morsel to eat for two long days.

"You poor little creature," said the field-mouse, who
was really a good old field-mouse, "come into my warm
room and dine with me." She was so pleased with Thumbelina that she said, "You are quite welcome to stay with
me all the winter, if you like; but you must keep my rooms
clean and neat, and tell me stories, for I like them very
much." So Thumbelina did all the field-mouse desired,
and was very comfortable on the whole.

One day the field-mouse said, "We shall have a visitor
soon. My neighbor pays me a visit once a week. He is better off than I am; he has large rooms, and wears a beautiful black velvet coat. If you could only have him for a husband, you would be well provided for indeed. But he is
blind, so you must tell him the prettiest stories you
know."

But Thumbelina did not feel at all interested in this
neighbor, for he was a mole. However, he came and paid
his visit, dressed in his black velvet coat.

"He is very rich and learned, and his house is twenty
times larger than mine," said the field-mouse.

He was rich and learned, no doubt, but he always spoke
slightingly of the sun and the pretty flowers, because he
had never seen them. Thumbelina was obliged to sing to
him, "Lady-bird, lady-bird, fly away home," and many

other pretty songs. And the mole fell in love with her sweet voice. A short time before, he had dug a long passage under the earth, which led from the dwelling of the field-mouse to his own, and the field-mouse and Thumbelina had permission to walk whenever they liked. He warned them not to be afraid of a dead bird that lay in the passage. The mole took a piece of phosphorescent wood in his mouth; it shone like fire in the dark and he led them through the long, dark passage. When they came to the spot where the dead bird lay, the mole pushed his broad nose through the ceiling, so as to make a large hole, through which the daylight shone into the passage. In the middle of the floor lay a dead swallow, his beautiful wings folded close to his sides, his feet and his head drawn up under his feathers. It made little Thumbelina very sad to see it, she so loved the little birds who had sung and twittered for her so beautifully all summer. But the mole pushed it aside with his crooked legs, and said, "He will sing no more now. How miserable it must be to be born a little bird! I am thankful that none of my children will ever be birds."

"Yes," exclaimed the field-mouse. "What is the use of his twittering, for when winter comes he must either starve or be frozen to death. Still, birds are very high bred."

Thumbelina said nothing; but when the two others had turned their backs on the bird, she stooped down and stroked the soft feathers of his head, and kissed the closed eyelids. "Perhaps this was the very one who sang to me so sweetly in the summer," she said; "and how much pleasure you gave me, you dear, pretty bird."

The mole now stopped up the hole through which the daylight shone, and led the ladies home again. But during the night Thumbelina could not sleep, so she got out of bed and wove a large, beautiful rug of hay. She carried it to the dead bird, and spread it over him, with some down from the flowers which she had found in the field-mouse's room. It was as soft as wool, and she spread some of it on each side of the bird, so that he might lie warmly in the cold earth.

"Farewell, pretty bird," said she, "farewell and thank you for your sweet singing through the summer, when all the trees were green, and the warm sun shone upon us." Then she laid her head on the bird's breast, but she was startled, for it seemed as if something inside the bird went "thump, thump." It was the bird's heart. He was not really dead, only numbed with the cold, and the warmth was restoring him to life.

In autumn, all the swallows fly away to warm countries, but if one happens to linger, the cold seizes it, it falls and remains where it fell, until the cold snow covers it. Thumbelina trembled; she was quite frightened, for the bird was large, a great deal larger than herself—she was only an inch high. But she took courage, laid the wool more thickly over the poor swallow, and then brought a leaf which she had used for her own counterpane, and laid it over the head of the poor bird.

The next night she again stole out to see him. He was alive but very weak; he could only open his eyes for a moment to look at Thumbelina, who stood holding a piece of phosphorescent wood in her hand, for she had no other lantern.

"Thank you, pretty child," said the sick swallow; "I have been so nicely warmed, that I shall be strong again and able to fly about in the warm sunshine."

"Oh," said she, "it is cold outdoors now; it snows and freezes. Stay in your warm bed! I will take care of you!"

She brought the swallow some water in a flower-leaf, and, after he had drunk, he told her that he had wounded one of his wings in a thorn-bush, and could not fly as fast as the others, who were soon far away on their journey to warm countries. At last he had fallen and could remember no more, nor how he came where she had found him. The whole winter the swallow remained underground, and Thumbelina nursed him with care and love. Neither the mole nor the field-mouse knew anything about it, for they did not like swallows.

The spring came, and the sun warmed the earth. Then the swallow bade farewell to Thumbelina, and she opened the hole which the mole had made in the ceiling. The sun shone in upon them so beautifully, that the swallow asked her if she would go with him; she could sit on his back, he said, and he would fly away with her into the green woods. But Thumbelina knew it would make the field-mouse sad if she left her that way, so she said, "No, I cannot."

"Farewell, then, farewell, you good, pretty little girl," said the swallow and flew out into the sunshine.

Thumbelina looked after him, and the tears rose in her eyes for she was very fond of the swallow.

"Tweet, tweet," sang the bird, flying out into the green woods. Thumbelina felt very sad. She was not allowed to go out into the warm sunshine. The corn which had been sown in the field over the house of the field-mouse had grown high into the air; it was a thick wood to Thumbelina, who was only an inch high.

"You are going to be married, Thumbelina," said the field-mouse. "My neighbor has asked for you. What good fortune for a poor child like you! Now we will make your wedding clothes. They must be both woolen and linen. Nothing must be wanting when you are the mole's wife."

Thumbelina had to turn the spinning wheel, and the field-mouse hired four spiders, who were to weave day and night. Every evening the mole visited her, and was always speaking of the time when the summer would be over. Then he would keep his wedding-day with Thumbelina; but now the heat of the sun was so great that it burned the earth, and made it quite hard, like a stone. As soon as the summer was over, the wedding should take place.

But Thumbelina was not happy; for she did not like the tiresome mole. Every morning when the sun rose, and every evening when it went down, she would creep out at the door, and as the wind blew aside the leaves of the corn, so that she could see the blue sky, she thought how beautiful and bright it seemed out there, and wished so much to see her dear swallow again.

When autumn arrived, Thumbelina's outfit was ready, and the field-mouse said, "In four weeks the wedding must take place."

Then Thumbelina cried, and said she did not want to marry the tiresome mole.

"Nonsense," replied the field-mouse. "Don't be foolish. He is a very handsome mole; the queen herself does not wear more beautiful velvets and furs. His kitchens and cellars are quite full. You ought to be thankful for such good fortune."

So the wedding-day was fixed, and the mole was to take Thumbelina to live with him, deep under the earth, and never again to see the warm sun, because he did not like it. The field-mouse had given her permission to stand at the door before she left.

"Farewell, bright sun," she cried, stretching out her arm towards it and she walked a short distance from the house, for the corn had been cut and only the dry stubble was left in the fields. "Farewell, farewell," she repeated, twining her arm round a little red flower. "Greet the little swallow from me, if you should see him again."

"Tweet, tweet," sounded over her head. She looked up, and there was the swallow himself flying close by. As soon as he spied Thumbelina, he was delighted. She told him how she was to marry the ugly mole, and how unhappy she felt that she must live always beneath the earth, and never see the bright sun any more. And as she told him, she wept.

"Cold winter is coming," said the swallow, "and I am going to fly away into warmer countries. Will you go with me? You can sit on my back, and fasten yourself on with your sash. Then we can fly away from the ugly mole and his gloomy home—far away, over the mountains, to warm countries, where the sun shines more brightly than here; where it is always summer, and the flowers are always in bloom. Fly now with me, dear little Thumbelina—you who saved my life when I lay frozen in that dark, dreary passage."

"Yes, I will go with you," said Thumbelina. She seated herself on the bird's back, with her feet on his outstretched wings, and tied her girdle to one of his strongest feathers.

Then the swallow rose in the air, and flew over forest and over sea, high above the highest mountains, covered with snow that never melts. Thumbelina would have been frozen in the cold air, but she crept under the bird's warm feathers, keeping her little head uncovered, so that she might admire the beautiful lands over which they passed. At length they reached the warm countries, where the sun shines more brightly, and the sky seems much higher above the earth. Here, on the hedges, and by the wayside, grew purple, green, and white grapes, and lemons and oranges hung from trees in the woods; the air was fragrant with myrtles and orange blossoms. Beautiful children ran along the country lanes, playing with gay butterflies; and as the swallow flew farther and farther, every place appeared still more lovely.

At last they came to a blue lake, and by the side of it, shaded by trees of the deepest green, stood a palace of dazzling white marble, built in ancient times. Vines clustered round its lofty pillars, and at the top were many swallows' nests; one of these was the home of the swallow who carried Thumbelina.

"This is my house," said the swallow; "but you would not be comfortable in it. Choose one of those lovely flowers, and I will put you down upon it, and then you shall have everything that you can wish to make you happy."

"That will be delightful," said Thumbelina, clapping her little hands.

A marble pillar had fallen to the ground, and lay there broken into three pieces. Between these pieces grew most beautiful large white flowers. The swallow flew down with Thumbelina, and placed her on one of the broad leaves. How astonished she was to see, in the middle of the flower, a tiny little man, as white and transparent as if he had been made of crystal! He had a gold crown on his head, and delicate wings at his shoulders, and was not much larger than Thumbelina herself. He was the angel of the flower; for a tiny man or a tiny woman dwells in every flower; and this was the king of them all.

"Oh, how beautiful he is!" whispered Thumbelina to the swallow.

The little prince was at first quite frightened at the bird, who was like a giant, compared to such a delicate little creature as himself; but when he saw Thumbelina, he was delighted. She was the prettiest little maid he had ever seen. He took the gold crown from his head, and placed it on hers, and asked her name, and if she would be his queen of all the flowers.

So she said, "Yes," to the handsome prince. Then all the flowers opened, and out of each came a little lady or a tiny lord, all so pretty that it was a pleasure to look at them. Each of them brought Thumbelina a present. The best gift was a pair of beautiful wings, which had belonged to a large white fly. They were fastened to Thumbelina's shoulders, so that she might fly from flower to flower. Then there was much rejoicing, and the little swallow, who sat above them, in his nest, was asked to sing a wedding song, which he did as well as he could; but in his heart he felt sad, for he was very fond of Thumbelina, and would have liked never to part from her again.

"You must not be called Thumbelina any more," said the spirit of the flowers to her. "It is an ugly name, and you are so very pretty. We will call you May."

"Farewell, farewell," said the swallow, as he left the warm countries, to fly back into Denmark. There he had a nest over the window of a house in which dwelt the man who wrote this story. The swallow sang, "Tweet, tweet," and from his song came the whole story.

The Little Match Girl

IT was terribly cold; it snowed and was already almost dark, and evening came on, the last evening of the year. In the cold and gloom a poor little girl, bare headed and barefoot, was walking through the streets. When she left her own house she certainly had had slippers on; but of what use were they? They were very big slippers, and her mother had used them till then, so big were they. The little maid lost them as she slipped across the road, where two carriages were rattling by terribly fast. One slipper was not to be found again, and a boy had seized the other, and run away with it. He thought he could use it very well as a cradle, some day when he had children of his own. So now the little girl went with her little naked feet, which were quite red and blue with the cold. In an old apron she carried a number of matches, and a bundle of them in her hand. No one had bought anything of her all day, and no one had given her a farthing.

Shivering with cold and hunger she crept along, a picture of misery, poor little girl! The snowflakes covered her long fair hair, which fell in pretty curls over her neck; but she did not think of that now. In all the windows lights were shining, and there was a glorious smell of roast goose, for it was New Year's Eve. Yes, she thought of that!

In a corner formed by two houses, one of which projected beyond the other, she sat down, cowering. She had drawn up her little feet, but she was still colder, and she did not dare to go home, for she had sold no matches, and did not bring a farthing of money. From her father she would certainly receive a beating, and besides, it was cold at home, for they had nothing over them but a roof through which the wind whistled, though the largest rents had been stopped with straw and rags.

Her little hands were almost benumbed with the cold. Ah! a match might do her good, if she could only draw one from the bundle, and rub it against the wall, and warm her hands at it. She drew one out. R-r-atch! how it sputtered and burned! It was a warm bright flame, like a little candle, when she held her hands over it; it was a wonderful little light! It really seemed to the little girl as if she sat before a great polished stove, with bright brass feet and a brass cover. How the fire burned! how comfortable it was! but the little flame went out, the stove vanished, and she had only the remains of the burned match in her hand.

A second was rubbed against the wall. It burned up, and when the light fell upon the wall it became transparent like a thin veil, and she could see through it into the room. On the table a snow-white cloth was spread; upon it stood a shining dinner service; the roast goose smoked gloriously stuffed with apples and dried plums. And what was still more splendid to behold, the goose hopped down from the dish, and waddled along the floor, with a knife and fork in its breast, to the little girl. Then the match went out, and only the thick, damp, cold wall was before her. She lighted another match. Then she was sitting under a beautiful Christmas tree; it was greater and more ornamented than the one she had seen through the glass door at the rich merchant's. Thousands of candles burned upon the green branches, and colored pictures like those in the print shops looked down upon them. The little girl stretched forth her hand towards them; then the match went out. The Christmas lights mounted higher. She saw them now as stars in the sky: one of them fell down, forming a long line of fire.

"Now some one is dying," thought the little girl, for her old grandmother, the only person who had loved her, and who was now dead, had told her that when a star fell down a soul mounted up to God.

She rubbed another match against the wall; it became bright again, and in the brightness the old grandmother stood clear and shining, mild and lovely.

"Grandmother!" cried the child, "Oh! take me with you! I know you will go when the match is burned out. You will vanish like the warm fire, the warm food, and the great glorious Christmas tree!"

And she hastily rubbed the whole bundle of matches, for she wished to hold her grandmother fast. And the matches burned with such a glow that it became brighter than in the middle of the day; grandmother had never been so large or so beautiful. She took the little girl in her arms, and both flew in brightness and joy above the earth, very, very high, and up there was neither cold, nor hunger, nor care—they were with God!

But in the corner, leaning against the wall, sat the poor girl with red cheeks and smiling mouth, frozen to death on the last evening of the Old Year. The New Year's sun rose upon a little corpse! The child sat there, stiff and cold, with the matches of which one bundle was burned. "She wanted to warm herself," the people said. No one imagined what a beautiful thing she had seen, and in what glory she had gone in with her grandmother to the New Year's Day.

The Nightingale

IN China, the emperor is a Chinaman, and all the people around him are Chinamen, too. It is many years since the story I am going to tell you happened, but that is all the more reason for telling it, lest it should be forgotten. The emperor's palace was the most beautiful thing in the world; it was made entirely of the finest porcelain, very costly, but at the same time so fragile that it could only be touched with the very greatest care. There were the most extraordinary flowers to be seen in the garden; the most beautiful ones had little silver bells tied to them, which tinkled perpetually, so that one could not pass the flowers without looking at them. Every little detail in the garden had been most carefully thought out, and it was so big, that even the gardener himself did not know where it ended. If one went on walking, one came to beautiful woods with lofty trees and deep lakes. The wood extended to the sea, which was deep and blue, deep enough for large ships to sail right up under the branches of the trees. Among these trees lived a nightingale, which sang so deliciously, that even the poor fisherman who had plenty of other things to do, lay still to listen to it, when he was out at night drawing in his nets. "Heavens, how beautiful it is!" he said, but then he had to attend to his business and forgot it. The next night when he heard it again he would again exclaim, "Heavens, how beautiful it is!"

Travelers came to the emperor's capital, from every

country in the world; they admired everything very much, especially the palace and the gardens, but when they heard the nightingale they all said, "This is better than anything!"

When they got home they described it, and the learned ones wrote many books about the town, the palace and the garden, but nobody forgot the nightingale, it was always put above everything else. Those among them who were poets wrote the most beautiful poems, all about the nightingale in the woods by the deep blue sea. These books went all over the world, and in course of time, some of them reached the emperor. He sat in his golden chair reading and reading, and nodding his head, well pleased to hear such beautiful descriptions of the town, the palace and the garden. "But the nightingale is the best of all," he read.

"What is this?" said the emperor. "The nightingale? Why, I know nothing about it. Is there such a bird in my kingdom, and in my own garden into the bargain, and I have never heard of it? Imagine my having to discover this from a book!"

Then he called his gentleman-in-waiting, who was so grand that when anyone of a lower rank dared to speak to him, or to ask him a question, he would only answer "P," which means nothing at all.

"There is said to be a very wonderful bird called a nightingale here," said the emperor. "They say that it is better than anything else in all my great kingdom! Why have I never been told anything about it?"

"I have never heard it mentioned," said the gentleman-in-waiting. "It has never been presented at court."

"I wish it to appear here this evening to sing to me," said the emperor. "The whole world knows what I am possessed of, and I know nothing about it!"

"I have never heard it mentioned before," said the gentleman-in-waiting. "I will seek it, and I will find it!" But where was it to be found? The gentleman-in-waiting ran upstairs and downstairs and in and out of all the rooms and corridors. No one of all those he met had ever heard anything about the nightingale; so the gentleman-in-waiting ran back to the emperor, and said that it must be a myth, invented by the writers of the books. "Your imperial majesty must not believe everything that is written; books are often mere inventions, even if they do not belong to what we call the black art!"

"But this book was sent to me by the powerful Emperor of Japan, so it can't be untrue. I will hear this nightingale; I insist upon its being here to-night. I extend my most gracious protection to it, and if it is not forthcoming, I will have the whole court trampled upon after supper!"

"Tsing-pe!" said the gentleman-in-waiting, and away he ran again, up and down all the stairs, in and out of all the rooms and corridors; half the court ran with him, for they none of them wished to be trampled on. There was much questioning about this nightingale, which was known to all the outside world, but to no one at court. At last they found a poor little maid in the kitchen. She said, "Oh heavens, the nightingale? I know it very well. Yes, indeed it can sing. Every evening I am allowed to take broken meat to my poor sick mother: she lives down by the shore. On my way back, when I am tired, I rest a while in the wood, and then I hear the nightingale. Its song brings the tears into my eyes, I feel as if my mother were kissing me!"

"Little kitchen maid," said the gentleman-in-waiting, "I will procure you a permanent position in the kitchen and permission to see the emperor dining, if you will take us to the nightingale. It is commanded to appear at court to-night."

Then they all went out into the wood where the nightingale usually sang. Half the court was there. As they were going along at their best pace a cow began to bellow.

"Oh!" said a young courtier, "there we have it. What wonderful power for such a little creature; I have certainly heard it before."

"No, those are the cows bellowing, we are a long way yet from the place."

Then the frogs began to croak in the marsh.

"Beautiful!" said the Chinese chaplain; "it is just like the tinkling of church bells."

"No, those are the frogs!" said the little kitchen maid. "But I think we shall soon hear it now!"

Then the nightingale began to sing.

"There it is!" said the little girl. "Listen, listen, there it sits!" and she pointed to a little gray bird up among the branches.

"Is it possible?" said the gentleman-in-waiting. "I should never have thought it was like that. How common it looks. Seeing so many grand people must have frightened all its colors away."

"Little nightingale!" called the kitchen maid quite loud, "our gracious emperor wishes to hear you sing to him!"

"With the greatest pleasure!" said the nightingale, warbling away in the most delightful fashion.

"It is just like crystal bells," said the gentleman-in-waiting. "Look at its little throat, how active it is. It is extraordinary that we have never heard of it before! I am sure it will be a great success at court!"

"Shall I sing again to the emperor?" said the nightingale, who thought he was present.

"My precious little nightingale," said the gentleman-in-waiting, "I have the honor to command your attendance at a court festival to-night, where you will charm his gracious majesty the emperor with your fascinating singing."

"It sounds best among the trees," said the nightingale, but it went with them willingly when it heard that the emperor wished it.

The palace had been brightened up for the occasion. The walls and the floors, which were all of china, shone by the light of many thousand golden lamps. The most beautiful flowers, all of the tinkling kind, were arranged in the corridors; there was hurrying to and fro, and one's ears were full of the tinkling. In the middle of the large reception room, where the emperor sat, a golden rod had been fixed, on which the nightingale was to perch. The whole court was assembled, and the little kitchen maid had been permitted to stand behind the door, as she now had the actual title of cook. They were all dressed in their best; everybody's eyes were turned towards the little gray bird at which the emperor was nodding. The nightingale sang delightfully, and the tears came into the emperor's eyes, nay, they rolled down his cheeks. The nightingale sang more beautifully than ever; its notes touched all hearts. The emperor was charmed, and said the nightingale should have his gold slipper to wear round its neck. But the nightingale declined with thanks, it had already been sufficiently rewarded.

"I have seen tears in the eyes of the emperor, that is my richest reward. The tears of an emperor have a wonderful power! God knows I am sufficiently recompensed!" and then it again burst into its sweet heavenly song.

"That is the most delightful coquetting I have ever seen!" said the ladies, and they took some water into their mouths to try and make the same gurgling when anyone spoke to them, thinking so to equal the nightingale. Even the lackeys and the chambermaids announced that they were satisfied, and that is saying a great deal, they are always the most difficult people to please. Yes, indeed, the nightingale had made a sensation. It was to stay at court now, and to have its own cage, as well as liberty to walk out twice a day, and once in the night. It always had twelve footmen, each one holding a ribbon which was tied round its leg. There was not much pleasure in an outing of that sort.

The whole town talked about the marvelous bird, and if two people met, one said to the other "Night," and the other answered "Gale," and then they sighed, perfectly understanding each other. Eleven cheese-mongers' children were named for it, but they had not a voice among them.

One day a large parcel came for the emperor, outside was written the word "Nightingale."

"Here we have another new book about this celebrated

bird," said the emperor. But it was no book, it was a little work of art in a box, an artificial nightingale, exactly like the living one, but it was studded all over with diamonds, rubies, and sapphires.

When the bird was wound up, it could sing one of the songs the real one sang, and it wagged its tail which glittered with silver and gold. A ribbon was tied round its neck on which was written, "The Emperor of Japan's nightingale is very poor, compared to the Emperor of China's."

Everybody said, "Oh, how beautiful!" And the person who brought the artificial bird immediately received the title of Imperial Nightingale-Carrier in Chief.

"Now, they must sing together. What a duet that will be!"

Then they had to sing together, but they did not get on very well, for the real nightingale sang in its own way, and the artificial one could only sing waltzes.

"There is no fault in that," said the music master; "it is perfectly in time and correct in every way!"

Then the artificial bird had to sing alone. It was just as great a success as the real one, besides it was so much prettier to look at; it glittered like bracelets and breast-pins.

It sang the same tune three and thirty times over, and yet it was not tired; people would willingly have heard it from the beginning again, but the emperor said that the real one must have a turn now—but where was it? No one had noticed that it had flown out of the open window, back to its own green woods.

"But what is the meaning of this?" said the emperor.

All the courtiers railed at it, and said it was a most ungrateful bird.

"We have got the best bird, though," said they, and then the artificial bird had to sing again, and this was the thirty-fourth time they heard the same tune, but they did not know it thoroughly even yet; it was so difficult.

The music master praised the bird tremendously, and

insisted that it was much better than the real nightingale, not only as regarded the outside with all the diamonds, but the inside, too.

"Because you see, my ladies and gentlemen, and the emperor before all, in the real nightingale you never know what you will hear, but in the artificial one everything is decided beforehand! So it is, and so it must remain, it can't be otherwise. You can account for things, you can open it and show the human ingenuity in arranging the waltzes, how they go, and how one note follows upon another!"

"Those are exactly my opinions," they all said, and the music master got leave to show the bird to the public, next Sunday. They might also hear it sing, said the emperor. So they heard it, and all became as enthusiastic over it as if they had drunk themselves merry on tea—a thoroughly Chinese habit.

Then they all said, "Oh," and stuck their forefingers in the air and nodded their heads; but the poor fishermen who had heard the real nightingale said, "It sounds very nice, and it is very like the real one, but there is something wanting, we don't know what." The real nightingale was banished from the kingdom.

The artificial bird had its place on a silken cushion, close to the emperor's bed: all the presents it had received of gold and precious jewels were scattered round it. Its title had risen to be "Chief Imperial Singer of the Bed-Chamber," in rank number one, on the left side; for the emperor reckoned that side the important one, where the heart was seated. Even an emperor's heart is on the left side. The music master wrote five and twenty volumes about the artificial bird; the treatise was very long, and written in all the most difficult Chinese characters. Everybody said they had read and understood it, for otherwise they would have been reckoned stupid and then their bodies would have been trampled upon.

Things went on in this way for a whole year. The emperor, the court, and all the other Chinamen knew every little gurgle in the song of the artificial bird by heart; but they liked it all the better for this, and they could all join in the song themselves. Even the street boys sang "zizizi" and "cluck, cluck, cluck," and the emperor sang it, too.

But, one evening, when the bird was singing its best, and the emperor was lying in bed listening to it, something gave way inside the bird with a "whizz." Then a spring burst; "whirr" went all the wheels and the music stopped. The emperor jumped out of bed and sent for his private physicians, but what good could they do? Then they sent for the watchmaker, and after a good deal of talk and examination, he got the works to go again, somehow; but he said it would have to be saved as much as possible, because it was so worn out, and he could not renew the works so as to be sure of the tune. This was a great blow! They only dared to let the artificial bird sing once a year, and hardly that; but then the music master made a little speech using all the most difficult words. He said it was just as good as ever, and his saying made it so.

Five years now passed, and then a great grief came upon the nation, for they were all very fond of their emperor. It was said he was ill and could not live. A new emperor was already chosen, and people stood about in the street, and asked the gentleman-in-waiting how their emperor was going on.

"P," answered he, shaking his head.

The emperor lay pale and cold in his gorgeous bed. The courtiers thought he was dead, and they all went off to pay their respects to their new emperor. The lackeys ran off to talk matters over, and the chambermaids gave a great coffee party. Cloth had been laid down in all the rooms and corridors so as to deaden the sounds of footsteps, so it was very, very quiet. But the emperor was not dead yet. He lay stiff and pale in the gorgeous bed with its velvet hangings and heavy golden tassels. There was an open window high above him, and the moon streamed in upon the emperor, and the artificial bird beside him.

The poor emperor could hardly breathe; he seemed to

have a weight on his chest. He opened his eyes and saw that it was Death sitting upon his chest, wearing his golden crown. In one hand he held the emperor's golden sword, and in the other his imperial banner. Round about, from among the folds of the velvet hangings peered many curious faces, some were hideous, others gentle and pleasant. They were all the emperor's good and bad deeds, which now looked him in the face when Death was weighing him down.

"Do you remember that?" whispered one after the other. "Do you remember this?" and they told him so many things, that the perspiration poured down his face.

"I never knew that," said the emperor. "Music, music, sound the great Chinese drums!" he cried, "that I may not hear what they are saying." But they went on and on, and Death sat nodding his head, just like a Chinaman, at everything that was said.

"Music, music!" shrieked the emperor. "You precious little golden bird, sing, sing! I have loaded you with precious stones, and even hung my own golden slipper round your neck. Sing, I tell you, sing!"

But the bird stood silent, there was nobody to wind it up, so of course it could not go. Death continued to fix the great empty sockets of its eyes upon the emperor, and all was silent, so terribly silent.

Suddenly, close to the window, there was a burst of lovely song; it was the living nightingale, perched on a branch outside. It had heard of the emperor's need, and had come to bring comfort and hope to him. And as it sang, the faces round the emperor became fainter and fainter, and the blood coursed with fresh vigor in his veins and through his feeble limbs. Even Death himself listened to the song and said, "Go on, little nightingale, go on!"

"Yes, if you give me the gorgeous golden sword; yes, if you give me the imperial banner; yes, if you give me the emperor's crown."

And Death gave back each of these treasures for a song, and the nightingale went on singing. It sang about the quiet churchyard, where the roses bloom, where the elder flower scents the air, and where the fresh grass is ever moistened anew by the tears of the mourner. This song brought to Death a longing for his own garden, and like a cold gray mist, he passed out of the window.

"Thanks, thanks!" said the emperor; "you heavenly little bird, I know you! I banished you from my kingdom, and yet you have charmed the evil visions away from my bed by your song, and even Death away from my heart! How can I ever repay you?"

"You have rewarded me," said the nightingale. "I brought the tears to your eyes, the very first time I ever sang to you, and I shall never forget it! Those are the jewels which gladden the heart of a singer. But sleep now, and wake up fresh and strong! I will sing to you!"

Then it sang again, and the emperor fell into a sweet refreshing sleep. The sun shone in at his window, when he woke fresh and well; none of his attendants had yet come back to him, for they thought he was dead, but the nightingale still sat there singing.

"You must always stay with me!" said the emperor. "You shall only sing when you like, and I will break the artificial bird into a thousand pieces!"

"Don't do that!" said the nightingale, "it did all the good it could! Keep it as you have always done! I can't build my nest and live in this palace, but let me come whenever I like, then I will sit on the branch in the evening and sing to you. I will sing to cheer you and to make you thoughtful, too; I will sing to you of the happy ones, and of those that suffer; I will sing about the good and the evil, which are kept hidden from you. The little singing bird flies far and wide, to the poor fisherman and the peasant's home, to numbers who are far from you and your court. I love your heart more than your crown, and yet there is an odor of sanctity round the crown, too!—I will come, and I will sing to you!—But you must promise me one thing!"—

"Everything!" said the emperor, who stood there in his

imperial robes which he had just put on, and he held the sword heavy with gold upon his heart.

"One thing I ask you! Tell no one that you have a little bird who tells you everything. It will be better so!"

Then the nightingale flew away. The attendants came in to see their dead emperor, and there he stood, bidding them "Good-morning!"

The Snow Queen

A Tale in Seven Stories

FIRST STORY

THIS is about a mirror and its fragments. Now we are about to begin and when we get to the end of the story, you will know more than you do now about a very wicked hobgoblin. He was one of the worst kind; in fact he was a real demon. One day, he was in a high state of delight because he had invented a mirror with this peculiarity, that every good and pretty thing reflected in it shrank away to almost nothing. On the other hand, every bad and good-for-nothing thing stood out and looked its worst. The most beautiful landscapes reflected in it looked like boiled spinach, and the best people became hideous, or else they were upside down and had no bodies. Their faces were distorted beyond recognition, and if they had even one freckle it appeared to spread all over the nose and mouth. The demon thought this immensely amusing. If a good thought passed through anyone's mind, it turned to a grin in the mirror, and this caused real delight to the demon. All the scholars in the demon's school, for he kept a school, reported that a miracle had taken place. Now for the first time it had become possible to see what the world and mankind were really like. They ran about all over with the mirror, till at last there was not a country or person which had not been seen in this distorting mirror. They even wanted to fly up to heaven with it to mock the angels; but the higher they flew, the more it grinned, so much so that they could hardly hold it, and at last it slipped out of their hands and fell to earth, shivered into hundreds of millions and billions of bits. Even then it did more harm than ever. Some of these bits were not as big as a grain of sand, and these flew about all over the world, getting into people's eyes, and, once in, they stuck there, and distorted everything they looked at, or made them see everything that was amiss. Each tiniest grain of glass kept the same power as that possessed by the whole mirror. Some people even got a bit of glass into their hearts, and that was terrible, for the heart became like a lump of ice. Some of the fragments were so big that they were used for window panes, but it was not advisable to look at one's friends through these panes. Other bits were made into spectacles, and it was a bad business when people put on these spectacles meaning to be just. The bad demon laughed till he split his sides; it tickled him to see the mischief he had done. But some of these fragments were still left floating about the world, and you shall hear what happened to them.

SECOND STORY

ABOUT A LITTLE BOY AND A LITTLE GIRL

In a big town crowded with houses and people, where there is no room for gardens, people have to be content with flowers in pots instead. In one of these towns lived two children who managed to have something bigger than a flower pot for a garden. They were not brother and sister, but they were just as fond of each other as if they had been. Their parents lived opposite each other in two attic rooms. The roof of one house just touched the roof of the next one, with only a rain water gutter between them. They each had a little dormer window, and one only had to step over the gutter to get from one house to the other. Each of the parents had a large window-box, in which they grew pot herbs and a little rose tree. There was one in each box, and they both grew splendidly. It occurred to the parents to put the boxes across the gutter, from house to house, and they looked just like two banks of flowers. The pea vines hung down over the edges of the boxes, and the roses threw out long creepers which twined round the windows. It was almost like a green triumphal arch. The boxes were high, and the children knew they must not climb up on to them, but they were often allowed to have their little stools out under the rose trees, and there they had delightful games. Of course in the winter there was an end to these amusements. The windows were often covered with hoar frost. They would warm coppers on the stove and stick them on the frozen panes, where they made lovely peep-holes as round as possible. Then a bright eye would peep through these holes, one from each window. The little boy's name was Kay, and the little girl's Gerda.

In the summer they could reach each other with one bound, but in the winter they had to go down all the stairs in one house and up all the stairs in the other, and outside there were snow-drifts.

"Look! the white bees are swarming," said the old grandmother.

"Have they a queen bee, too?" asked the little boy, for he knew that there was a queen among the real bees.

"Yes, indeed they have," said the grandmother. "She flies where the swarm is thickest. She is the biggest of them all, and she never remains on the ground. She always flies up again to the sky. Many a winter's night she flies through the streets and peeps in at the windows, and then the ice freezes on the panes into wonderful patterns like flowers."

"Oh yes, we have seen that," said both children, and then they knew it was true.

"Can the Snow Queen come in here?" asked the little girl.

"Just let her come," said the boy, "and I will put her on the stove, where she will melt."

But the grandmother smoothed his hair and told him more stories.

In the evening when little Kay was at home and half un-dressed, he crept up on the chair by the window, and peeped out of the little hole. A few snowflakes were falling, and one of these, the biggest, remained on the edge of the window-box. It grew bigger and bigger, till it became the figure of a woman, dressed in the finest white gauze, which appeared to be made of millions of starry flakes. She was delicately lovely, but all ice, glittering, daz-zling ice. Still she was alive, her eyes shone like two bright stars, but there was no rest or peace in them. She nodded to the window and waved her hand. The little boy was frightened and jumped down off the chair, and then he fancied that a big bird flew past the window.

The next day was bright and frosty, and then came the thaw—and after that the spring. The sun shone, green buds began to appear, the swallows built their nests, and people began to open their windows. The little children began to play in their garden on the roof again. The roses were in splendid bloom that summer; the little girl had learned a hymn, and there was something in it about roses, and that made her think of her own. She sang it to the little boy, and then he sang it with her—

> "Where roses deck the flowery vale,
> There, Infant Jesus, we Thee hail!"

The children took each other by the hands, kissed the roses, and rejoiced in God's bright sunshine, and spoke to it as if the Child Jesus were there. What lovely summer days they were, and how delightful it was to sit out under the fresh rose trees, which seemed never tired of blooming.

Kay and Gerda were looking at a picture book of birds and animals, one day—it had just struck five by the church clock—when Kay said, "Oh, something struck my heart, and I have got something in my eye!"

The little girl put her arms round his neck, he blinked his eye, there was nothing to be seen.

"I believe it is gone," he said. But it was not gone. It was one of those very grains of glass from the mirror, the magic mirror. You remember that horrid mirror, in which all good and great things reflected in it became small and mean, while the bad things were magnified, and every flaw became very apparent.

Poor Kay! a grain of it had gone straight to his heart, and would soon turn it to a lump of ice. He did not feel it any more, but it was still there.

"Why do you cry?" he asked; "it makes you look ugly; there's nothing the matter with me. How horrid!" he suddenly cried; "there's a worm in that rose, and that one is quite crooked; after all, they are nasty roses, and so are the boxes they are growing in!" He kicked the box and broke off two of the roses.

"What are you doing, Kay?" cried the little girl. When he saw her alarm, he broke off another rose, and then ran in, by his own window, and left the dear little Gerda alone.

When she next got out the picture book, he said it was only fit for babies in long clothes. When his grandmother told them stories, he always had a but—, and if he could manage it, he liked to get behind her chair, put on her spectacles and imitate her. He did it very well and people laughed at him. He was soon able to imitate every one in the street; he could make fun of all their peculiarities and failings. "He will turn out a clever fellow," said people. But it was all that bit of glass in his heart, that bit of glass in his eye, and it made him tease little Gerda, who was so devoted to him. He played quite different games now; he seemed to have grown older. One winter's day, when the snow was falling fast, he brought in a big magnifying glass; he held out the tail of his blue coat, and let the snowflakes fall upon it.

"Now look through the glass, Gerda!" he said; every snowflake was magnified, and looked like a lovely flower, or a sharply pointed star.

"Do you see how cleverly they are made," said Kay. "Much more interesting than looking at real flowers, and there is not a single flaw in them, they are perfect, if only they would not melt."

Shortly after, he appeared in his thick gloves, with his sledge on his back. He shouted right into Gerda's ear, "I have got leave to drive in the big square where the other boys play!" and away he went.

In the big square the bolder boys used to tie their little sledges to the farm carts and go a long way in this fashion. They had no end of fun over it. Just in the middle of their games, a big sledge came along; it was painted white and the occupant wore a white fur coat and cap. The sledge drove twice around the square, and Kay quickly tied his sledge on behind. Then off they went, faster, and faster, into the next street. The driver turned round and nodded to Kay in the most friendly way, just as if they knew each other. Every time Kay wanted to loose his sledge, the person nodded again, and Kay stayed where he was, and they drove right out through the town gates. Then the snow began to fall so heavily, that the little boy could not see a hand before him as they rushed along. He undid the cords and tried to get away from the big sledge, but it was no use, his little sledge stuck fast, and on they rushed, faster than the wind. He shouted aloud but nobody heard him and the sledge tore on through the snowdrifts. Every now and then it gave a bound, as if they were jumping over hedges and ditches. He was very much frightened, and he wanted to say his prayers, but he could only remember the multiplication tables.

The snowflakes grew bigger and bigger till at last they looked like big white chickens. All at once they sprang on one side, the big sledge stopped and the person who drove got up, coat and cap smothered in snow. It was a tall and upright lady, all shining white,—the Snow Queen herself.

"We have come along at a good pace," she said; "but it's cold enough to kill one; creep inside my bearskin coat."

She took him into the sledge by her, wrapped him in her furs, and he felt as if he were sinking into a snow-drift.

"Are you still cold?" she asked, and she kissed him on the forehead. Ugh! it was colder than ice, it went to his very heart, which was already more than half ice; he felt as if he were dying, but only for a moment, and then it seemed to have done him good, he no longer felt the cold.

"My sledge! don't forget my sledge!" He had almost forgotten it. It was tied to one of the white chickens which flew along behind them. The Snow Queen kissed Kay again, and then he forgot all about little Gerda, Grandmother, and all the others at home.

"Now I mustn't kiss you any more," she said, "or I should kiss you to death!"

Kay looked at her, she was so pretty; a cleverer, more beautiful face could hardly be imagined. She did not seem to be made of ice, now, as she was outside the window when she had waved her hand to him. In his eyes she was quite perfect, and he was not a bit afraid of her; he told her that he could do mental arithmetic, as far as fractions, and that he knew the number of square miles and the number of inhabitants of the country. She always smiled at him, and he then thought he surely did not know enough and he looked up into the wide expanse of heaven, into which they rose higher and higher as she flew with him on a dark cloud, while the storm surged around them, the wind ringing in their ears like well-known old songs.

They flew over the woods and lakes, over oceans and islands, the cold wind whistled down below them, the wolves howled, the black crows flew screaming over the sparkling snow, but up above, the moon shone bright and clear—and Kay looked at it all the long, long winter nights; in the day he slept at the Snow Queen's feet.

THIRD STORY

The Garden of the Woman Learned in Magic

But how was little Gerda getting on all this long time since Kay left her? She wondered where could he be? Nobody

knew, nobody could say anything about him. All that the
other boys knew was that they had seen him tie his little
sledge to a splendid big one which drove away down the
street and out of the town gates. Nobody knew where he
was, and many tears were shed; little Gerda cried long and
bitterly. At last, people said he was dead; he must have
fallen into the river which ran close by the town. Oh, what
long, dark, winter days those were!

At last the spring came and the sunshine.

"Kay is dead and gone," said little Gerda.

"I don't believe it," said the sunshine.

"He is dead and gone," she said to the swallows.

"We don't believe it," said the swallows, and at last little Gerda did not believe it, either.

"I will put on my new red shoes," she said one morning;
"those Kay never saw and I will go down to the river and
ask it about him!"

It was very early in the morning; she kissed the old
grandmother, who was still asleep, put on the red shoes
and went, quite alone, out by the gate to the river.

"Is it true that you have taken my little playfellow? I will
give you my red shoes if you will bring him back to me
again."

She thought the little ripples nodded in a curious way,
so she took off her red shoes, her most cherished pos-
sessions, and threw them both into the river. They fell
close by the shore, and were carried straight back to her
by the little wavelets. It seemed as if the river would not
accept her offering, as it had not taken little Kay.

She only thought she had not thrown them far enough,
so she climbed into a boat which lay among the rushes,
then she went right out to the further end of it, and threw
the shoes into the water again. But the boat was loose,
and her movements started it off, and it floated away from
the shore. She felt it moving and tried to get out, but before she reached the other end the boat was more than a
yard from the shore, and was floating away quite quickly.

Little Gerda was terribly frightened, and began to cry,

but nobody heard her except the sparrows, and they could not carry her ashore, but flew alongside, twittering as if to cheer her, "we are here, we are here." The boat floated rapidly away with the current; little Gerda sat quite still with only her stockings on; her little red shoes floated behind, but they could not catch up with the boat which drifted away faster and faster.

The banks on both sides were very pretty with beautiful flowers, fine old trees, and slopes dotted with sheep and cattle, but not a single person did she see.

"Perhaps the river is taking me to little Kay," thought Gerda, and that cheered her. She sat up and looked at the beautiful green banks for hours.

Then they came to a big cherry garden. There was a little house in it, with curious blue and red windows, it had a thatched roof, and two wooden soldiers stood outside, who presented arms as she sailed past. Gerda called out to them. She thought they were alive, but of course they did not answer; she was quite close to them, for the current drove the boat close to the bank. Gerda called out again, louder than before, and then an old, old woman came out of the house; she was leaning upon a big, hooked stick, and she wore a big sun hat, which was covered with beautiful painted flowers.

"You poor little child," said the old woman, "however were you driven out on this big, strong river into the wide, wide world alone?" Then she walked right into the water, and caught hold of the boat with her hooked stick and she drew it ashore, and lifted little Gerda out.

Gerda was delighted to be on dry land again, but she was a little bit frightened of the strange old woman.

"Come, tell me who you are, and how you got here," said she.

When Gerda had told her the whole story and asked her if she had seen Kay, the woman said she had not seen him, but that she expected him. Gerda must not be sad, she was to come and taste her cherries and see her flowers, which were more beautiful than any picture-book; each

one had a story to tell. Then she took Gerda by the hand,
they went into the little house, and the old woman locked
the door.

The windows were very high up, and they were red,
blue, and yellow; they threw a very curious light into the
room. On the table were quantities of the most delicious
cherries, of which Gerda had leave to eat as many as ever
she liked. While she was eating, the old woman combed
Gerda's hair with a golden comb, so that the hair curled,
and shone like gold round the pretty little face, which was
as sweet as a rose.

"I have long wanted a little girl like you!" said the old
woman. "You will see how well we shall get on together."
While she combed her hair, Gerda had forgotten all about
Kay, for the old woman was learned in the magic art, but
she was not a bad witch and only cast spells over people
for a little amusement. She wanted to keep Gerda. She
therefore went into the garden and waved her hooked
stick over all the rose-bushes, and however beautifully
they were flowering, all sank down into the rich black
earth without leaving a trace behind them. The old
woman was afraid that if Gerda saw the roses she would
be reminded of Kay, and would want to run away. Then
she took Gerda into the flower garden. What a delicious
scent there was! and every imaginable flower for every
season was in that lovely garden; no picture-book could
be brighter or more beautiful. Gerda jumped for joy and
played till the sun went down behind the tall cherry trees.
Then she was put into a lovely bed with rose-colored
silken coverings stuffed with violets; she slept and
dreamed as lovely dreams as any queen on her wedding
day.

The next day she played with the flowers in the garden
again—and many days passed in the same way. Gerda
knew every flower, but however many there were, she always thought there was one missing, but what it was she
did not know.

One day she was sitting, looking at the old woman's sun

hat with all its painted flowers, and the very prettiest one of them all was a rose. The old woman had forgotten her hat when she charmed the others away. This is the consequence of being absent-minded.

"What!" said Gerda, "are there no roses here?" and she sprang in among the flower beds and sought. But in vain! Her hot tears fell on the very places where the roses used to be; when the warm drops moistened the earth, the rose trees shot up again, just as full of bloom as when they sank. Gerda embraced the roses and kissed them, and then she thought of the lovely roses at home, and this brought the thought of little Kay.

"Oh, how I have been delayed," said the little girl. "I ought to have been looking for Kay! Don't you know where he is?" she asked the roses. "Do you think he is dead and gone?"

"He is not dead," said the roses. "For we have been down underground, you know, and all the dead people are there, but Kay is not among them."

"Oh, thank you!" said little Gerda, and then she went to the other flowers and looked into their cups and said, "Do you know where Kay is?"

But each flower stood in the sun and dreamed its own dreams. Little Gerda heard many of these, but never anything about Kay.

And what said the Tiger lilies?

"Do you hear the drum? rub-a-dub, it has only two notes, rub-a-dub, always the same. The wailing of women and the cry of the preacher. The Hindu woman in her long red garment stands on the pile, while the flames surround her and her dead husband. But the woman is only thinking of the living man in the circle round, whose eyes burn with a fiercer fire than that of the flames which consume the body. Do the flames of the heart die in the fire?"

"I understand nothing about that," said little Gerda.

"That is my story," said the Tiger lily.

"What does the convolvulus say?"

"An old castle is perched high over a narrow mountain

path, it is closely covered with ivy, almost hiding the old red walls, and creeping up leaf upon leaf right round the balcony where stands a beautiful maiden. She bends over the balustrade and looks eagerly up the road. No rose on its stem is fresher than she; no apple blossom wafted by the wind moves more lightly. Her silken robes rustle softly as she bends over and says, 'Will he never come?'"

"Is it Kay you mean?" asked Gerda.

"I am only talking about my own story, my dream," answered the convolvulus.

What said the little snowdrop?

"Between two trees a rope with a board is hanging; it is a swing. Two pretty little girls in snowy frocks and green ribbons fluttering on their hats are seated on it. Their brother, who is bigger than they are, stands up behind them; he has his arms round the ropes for supports, and holds in one hand a little bowl and in the other a clay pipe. He is blowing soap-bubbles. As the swing moves, the bubbles fly upwards in all their changing colors, the last one still hangs from the pipe swayed by the wind, and the swing goes on. A little black dog runs up, he is almost as light as the bubbles, he stands up on his hind legs and wants to be taken into the swing, but it does not stop. The little dog falls with an angry bark; they jeer at it; the bubble bursts. A swinging plank, a fluttering foam picture—that is my story!"

"I daresay what you tell me is very pretty, but you speak so sadly and you never mention little Kay."

What says the hyacinth?

"They were three beautiful sisters, all most delicate, and quite transparent. One wore a crimson robe, the other a blue, and the third was pure white. These three danced hand-in-hand, by the edge of the lake in the moonlight. They were human beings, not fairies of the wood. The fragrant air attracted them, and they vanished into the wood; here the fragrance was stronger still. Three coffins glide out of the wood towards the lake, and in them lie the maidens. The fireflies flutter lightly round them with their flickering little torches. Do these dancing maidens sleep, or are they dead? The scent of the flower says that they are corpses. The evening bell tolls their knell."

"You make me quite sad," said little Gerda; "your perfume is so strong it makes me think of those dead maidens. Oh, is little Kay really dead? The roses have been down underground, and they say no."

"Ding, dong," tolled the hyacinth bells; "we are not tolling for little Kay; we know nothing about him. We sing our song, the only one we know."

And Gerda went on to the buttercups shining among their dark green leaves.

"You are a bright little sun," said Gerda. "Tell me if you know where I shall find my little playfellow."

The buttercup shone brightly and returned Gerda's glance. What song could the buttercup sing? It would not be about Kay.

"God's bright sun shone into a little court on the first day of spring. The sunbeams stole down the neighboring white wall, close to which bloomed the first yellow flower of the season; it shone like burnished gold in the sun. An old woman had brought her armchair out into the sun; her granddaughter, a poor and pretty little maid-servant, had come to pay her a short visit, and she kissed her. There was gold, heart's gold, in the kiss. Gold on the lips, gold on the ground and gold above, in the early morning beams! Now that is my little story," said the buttercup.

"Oh, my poor old grandmother!" sighed Gerda. "She will be longing to see me, and grieving about me, as she did about Kay. But I shall soon go home again and take Kay with me. It is useless for me to ask the flowers about him. They only know their own stories, and have no information to give me."

Then she tucked up her little dress, so that she might run the faster, but the narcissus blossoms struck her on the legs as she jumped over them, so she stopped and said, "Perhaps you can tell me something."

She stooped down close to the flower and listened. What did it say?

"I can see myself, I can see myself," said the narcissus. "Oh, how sweet is my scent. Up there in an attic window stands a little dancing girl half dressed; first she stands on one leg, then on the other, and looks as if she would tread the whole world under her feet. She is only a delusion. She pours some water out of a teapot on to a bit of stuff that she is holding; it is her bodice. 'Cleanliness is a good thing,' she says. Her white dress hangs on a peg; it has been washed in the teapot, too, and dried on the roof. She puts it on, and wraps a saffron colored scarf round her neck, which makes the dress look whiter. See how high she carries her head, and all upon one stem. I see myself, I see myself!"

"I don't care a bit about all that," said Gerda; "it's no use telling me such stuff."

And then she ran to the end of the garden. The door was fastened, but she pressed the rusty latch, and it gave way. The door swung open, and little Gerda ran out with bare feet into the wide world. She looked back three times, but nobody came after her. She ran until she could run no further, and she sat down on a big stone. When she looked round she saw that the summer was over, it was quite late autumn. She would never have known it inside the beautiful garden, where the sun always shone, and the flowers of every season were always in bloom.

"Oh, how I have wasted my time," said little Gerda. "It is autumn. I must not rest any longer," and she got up to go on.

How weary and sore were her little feet, and everything around looked so cold and dreary. The long willow leaves were quite yellow. The damp mist fell off the trees like rain, one leaf dropped after another from the trees, and only the sloe-thorn still bore its fruit, but the sloes were sour and set one's teeth on edge. Oh, how gray and sad it looked, out in the wide world.

FOURTH STORY

PRINCE AND PRINCESS

Gerda was soon obliged to rest again. A big crow hopped on to the snow, just in front of her. It had been sitting looking at her for a long time and wagging its head. Now it said "Caw, caw; good-day, good-day," as well as it could; it meant to be kind to the little girl, and asked her where she was going, alone in the wide world.

Gerda understood the word "alone" and knew how much there was in it, and she told the crow the whole story of her life and adventures, and asked if it had seen Kay.

The crow nodded his head gravely and said, "Maybe I have, maybe I have."

"What, do you really think you have?" cried the little girl, nearly smothering him with her kisses.

"Gently, gently!" said the crow. "I believe it may have been Kay, but he has forgotten you by this time, I expect, for the princess."

"Does he live with a princess?" asked Gerda.

"Yes, listen!" said the crow. "But it is so difficult to speak your language. If you understand 'crow's language,'* I can tell you about it much better."

"No, I have never learned it," said Gerda; "but grandmother knew it, and used to speak it. If only I had learned it!"

"It doesn't matter," said the crow. "I will tell you as well as I can, although I may do it rather badly."

Then he told her what he had heard.

"In this kingdom where we are now," said he, "there lives a princess who is very clever. She has read all the newspapers in the world, and forgotten them again, so clever is she. One day, she was sitting on her throne,

---

*Children have a kind of language, or gibberish, formed by adding letters or syllables to every word, which is called "Crow's language."

which is not such an amusing thing to do either, they say,
and she began humming a tune, which happened to be

'Why should I not be married, oh why?'

'Why not, indeed?' said she. And she made up her mind to
marry, if she could find a husband who had an answer
ready when a question was put to him. She called all the
court ladies together, and when they heard what she
wanted, they were delighted.

"'I like that now,' they said. 'I was thinking the same
thing myself, the other day.'

"Every word I say is true," said the crow, "for I have a
tame sweetheart who goes about the palace whenever
she likes. She told me the whole story."

Of course his sweetheart was a crow, for "birds of a
feather flock together," and one crow always chooses another. The newspapers all came out immediately with
their borders of hearts and the princess's initials. They
gave notice that any young man who was handsome
enough might go to the palace to speak to the princess.
The one who spoke as if he were quite at home, and spoke
well, would be chosen by the princess as her husband.
"Yes, yes, you may believe me, it's as true as that I sit
here," said the crow. "The people came crowding in; there
was such running, and crushing, but no one was fortunate
enough to be chosen, either on the first day, or on the second. They could all of them talk well enough in the street,
but when they entered the castle gates, and saw the guard
in silver uniforms, and when they went up the stairs
through rows of lackeys in gold embroidered liveries,
their courage forsook them. When they reached the bril-
liantly lighted reception rooms, and stood in front of the
throne where the princess was seated, they could think of
nothing to say, they only echoed her last words, and of
course that was not what she wanted.

"It was just as if they had all taken some kind of sleeping powder, which made them lethargic; they did not re-
cover themselves until they got out into the street again,

and then they had plenty to say. There was quite a long line of them, reaching from the town gates up to the palace.

"I went to see them myself," said the crow. "They were hungry and thirsty, but they got nothing at the palace, not even as much as a glass of tepid water. Some of the wise ones had taken sandwiches with them, but they did not share them with their neighbors! They thought if the others went in to the princess looking hungry, that there would be more chance for themselves."

"But Kay, little Kay!" asked Gerda; "when did he come? Was he amongst the crowd?"

"Give me time, give me time! We are just coming to him. It was on the third day that a little personage came marching cheerfully along, without either carriage or horse. His eyes sparkled like yours, and he had beautiful long hair, but his clothes were very shabby."

"Oh, that was Kay!" said Gerda gleefully; "then I have found him!" and she clapped her hands.

"He had a little knapsack on his back!" said the crow.

"No, it must have been on his sledge; he had it with him when he went away!" said Gerda.

"It may be so," said the crow; "I did not look very particularly, but I know from my sweetheart, that when he entered the palace gates, and saw the life guards in their silver uniforms, and the lackeys on the stairs in their gold laced liveries, he was not the least bit abashed. He just nodded to them and said, 'It must be very tiresome to stand upon the stairs. I am going inside!' The rooms were blazing with lights. Privy councillors and excellencies without number were walking about barefoot carrying golden vessels; it was enough to make you solemn! His boots creaked fearfully too, but he wasn't a bit upset."

"Oh, I am sure that was Kay!" said Gerda; "I know he had a pair of new boots, I heard them creaking in grandmother's room."

"Yes, indeed they did creak!" said the crow. "But nothing daunted, he went straight up to the princess, who was sitting on a pearl, as big as a spinning wheel. Poor, simple boy! All the court ladies and their attendants, the courtiers, and their gentlemen, each attended by a page, were standing round. The nearer the door they stood, so much the greater was their haughtiness, till the footman's boy who always wore slippers and stood in the doorway, was almost too proud even to be looked at."

"It must be awful!" said little Gerda, "and yet Kay has won the princess!"

"If I had not been a crow, I should have taken her myself, notwithstanding that I am engaged. They say he spoke as well as I could have done myself, when I speak crow-language; at least so my sweetheart says. He was a picture of good looks and gallantry, and then, he had not come with any idea of wooing the princess, but simply to hear her wisdom. He admired her just as much as she admired him!"

"Indeed it was Kay then," said Gerda; "he was so clever he could do mental arithmetic up to fractions. Oh, won't you take me to the palace?"

"It's easy enough to talk," said the crow, "but how are we to manage it? I will talk to my tame sweetheart about it. She will have some advice to give us, I daresay, but I am bound to tell you that a little girl like you will never be admitted!"

"Oh, indeed I shall," said Gerda; "when Kay hears that I am here, he will come out at once to fetch me."

"Wait here for me by the stile," said the crow, then he wagged his head and flew off.

The evening had darkened in before he came back. "Caw, caw," he said, "she sends you greeting, and here is a little roll for you. She got it out of the kitchen where there is bread enough, and I daresay you are hungry! It is not possible for you to get into the palace. You have bare feet; the guards in silver and the lackeys in gold would never allow you to pass. But don't cry! We shall get you in, somehow; my sweetheart knows a little back staircase which leads up to the bedroom, and she knows where the key is kept."

So they went into the garden, into the great avenue where the leaves were, softly one by one; and when the palace lights went out, one after the other, the crow led little Gerda to the back door, which was ajar.

Oh, how Gerda's heart beat with fear and longing! It was just as if she was about to do something wrong, and yet she only wanted to know if this really was little Kay. Oh, it must be he, she thought, picturing to herself his clever eyes and his long hair. She could see his very smile when they used to sit under the rose trees at home. She thought he would be very glad to see her, and to hear what a long way she had come to find him, and to hear how sad they had all been at home when he did not come back. Oh, it was joy mingled with fear.

They had now reached the stairs, where the little lamp was burning on a shelf. There stood the tame sweetheart, twisting and turning her head to look at Gerda, who made a curtsey, as grandmother had taught her.

"My betrothed has spoken so charmingly to me about you, my little miss!" she said. "Your life, '*Vita*,' as it is called, is most touching! If you will take the lamp, I will go on in front. We shall take the straight road here, and we shall meet no one."

"It seems to me that someone is coming up behind us," said Gerda, as she fancied something rushed past her throwing a shadow on the walls—horses with flowing manes and slender legs—huntsmen, ladies and gentlemen on horseback.

"Oh, those are only the dreams!" said the crow. "They come to take the thoughts of the noble ladies and gentlemen out hunting. That's a good thing, for you will be able to see them all the better in bed. But don't forget, when you are taken into favor, that you show a grateful spirit."

"Now, there's no need to talk about that," said the crow from the woods.

They now came into the first apartment; it was hung

with rose-colored satin embroidered with flowers. Here again the dreams overtook them, but they flitted by so quickly that Gerda could not distinguish them. The apartments became one more beautiful than the other; they were enough to bewilder anybody. They now reached the bedroom. The ceiling was like a great palm with crystal leaves, and in the middle of the room were two beds, each like a lily hung from a golden stem. One was white, and in it lay the princess; the other was red, and there lay he whom Gerda had come to seek—little Kay! She bent aside one of the crimson leaves, and she saw a little brown neck. It was Kay! She called his name aloud, and held the lamp close to him. Again the dreams rushed through the room on horse-back—he awoke, turned his head—and it was not little Kay.

It was only the prince's neck which was like Kay's, but he was young and handsome. The princess peeped out of her lily-white bed, and asked what was the matter. Then little Gerda cried and told them all her story, and what the crows had done to help her.

"You poor little thing!" said the prince and princess. And they praised the crows, and said that they were not at all angry with them, but they must not do it again. Then they gave them a reward.

"Would you like your liberty?" said the princess, "or would you prefer permanent posts about the court as court crows with perquisites from the kitchen?"

Both crows curtsied and begged for the permanent posts, for they thought of their old age, and said "It was so good to have something for the old man," as they called it.

The prince got up and allowed Gerda to sleep in his bed, and he could not have done more. She folded her little hands, and thought "How good the people and the animals are"; then she shut her eyes and fell fast asleep. All the dreams came flying back again; this time they looked like angels, and they were dragging a little sledge with Kay sitting on it, and he nodded. But it was only a dream; so it all vanished when she woke.

Next day she was dressed in silk and velvet from head to foot; they asked her to stay at the palace and have a good time, but she only begged them to give her a little carriage and horse, and a little pair of boots, so that she might drive out into the wide world to look for Kay.

They gave her a pair of boots and a muff and she was beautifully dressed, and when she was ready to start, there before the door stood a new chariot of pure gold. The prince's and princess's coat-of-arms was emblazoned on it, and shone like a star. Coachman, footman, and outrider, for there was even an outrider, all wore golden crowns. The prince and princess themselves helped her into the carriage and wished her joy. The wood crow, who was now married, accompanied her for the first three miles. He sat beside Gerda for he could not ride with his back to the horses and the other crow stood at the door and flapped her wings. She did not go with them, for she suffered from headache since she had been a kitchen pensioner—the consequence of eating too much. The chariot was stored with sugar biscuits and there were fruit and ginger nuts under the seat. "Good-by, good-by," cried the prince and princess; little Gerda wept and the crow wept, too. At the end of the first few miles the crow said good-by, and this was the hardest parting of all. It flew up into a tree and flapped its big black wings as long as it could see the chariot which shone like the brightest sunshine.

FIFTH STORY

THE LITTLE ROBBER GIRL

They drove on through a dark wood, where the chariot lighted up the way and blinded the robbers by its glare; it was more than they could bear.

"It is gold, it is gold!" they cried, and darting forward, seized the horses, and killed the postillions, the coachman and footman. Then they dragged little Gerda out of the carriage.

"She is fat, and she is pretty. She has been fattened on nuts!" said the old robber woman, who had a long beard and eyebrows that hung down over her eyes. "She is as good as a fat lamb, and how nice she will taste!" She drew out her sharp knife as she said this; it glittered horribly. "Oh!" screamed the old woman at the same moment, for her little daughter had come up behind her, and she was biting her ear. She hung on her back, as wild and as savage a little animal as you could wish to find. "You bad, wicked child!" said the mother, but she was prevented from killing Gerda on this occasion.

"She shall play with me," said the little robber girl. "She shall give me her muff, and her pretty dress, and she shall sleep in my bed." Then she bit her mother again and made her dance. All the robbers laughed and said, "Look at her dancing with her cub!"

"I want to get into the carriage," said the little robber girl, and she always had her own way because she was so spoilt and stubborn. She and Gerda got into the carriage and then they drove over stubble and stones further and further into the wood. The little robber girl was as big as Gerda, but much stronger; she had broader shoulders, and darker skin, her eyes were quite black, with almost a melancholy expression. She put her arm around Gerda's waist and said:

"They sha'n't kill you as long as I don't get angry with you; you must surely be a princess!"

"No," said little Gerda, and then she told her all her adventures, and how fond she was of Kay.

The robber girl looked earnestly at her, gave a little nod, and said, "They sha'n't kill you, even if I am angry with you! I will do it myself." Then she dried Gerda's eyes, and stuck her own hands into the pretty muff, which was so soft and warm.

At last the chariot stopped; they were in the courtyard of a robbers' castle, the walls of which were cracked from top to bottom. Ravens and crows flew in and out of every hole, and big bulldogs, which each looked ready to devour somebody, jumped about as high as they could, but they did not bark, for it was not allowed. A big fire was burning in the middle of the stone floor of the smoky old hall. The smoke all went up to the ceiling where it had to find a way out for itself. Soup was boiling in a big cauldron over the fire, and hares and rabbits were roasting on the spits.

"You shall sleep with me and all my little pets to-night," said the robber girl.

When they had had something to eat and drink they went along to one corner which was spread with straw and rugs. There were nearly a hundred pigeons roosting overhead on the rafters and beams. They seemed to be asleep, but they fluttered about a little when the children came in.

"They are all mine," said the little robber girl, seizing one of the nearest. She held it by the legs and shook it till it flapped its wings. "Kiss it," she cried, dashing it at Gerda's face. "Those are the wood pigeons," she added, pointing to some laths fixed across a big hole high up on the walls. "They are a regular rabble; they would fly away directly if they were not locked in. And here is my old sweetheart Be," dragging forward a reindeer by the horn. It was tied up, and it had a bright copper ring around its neck. "We have to keep him close, too, or he would run off. Every single night I tickle his neck with my bright knife, he is so frightened of it." The little girl produced a long knife out of a hole in the wall and drew it across the reindeer's neck. The poor animal laughed and kicked, and the robber girl laughed and pulled Gerda down into the bed with her.

"Do you have that knife by you while you are asleep?" asked Gerda, looking rather frightened.

"I always sleep with a knife," said the little robber girl. "You never know what will happen. But now tell me again what you told me before about little Kay, and why you went out into the world." So Gerda told her all about it again, and the wood pigeons cooed up in their cage above them; the other pigeons were asleep. The little robber girl put her arm around Gerda's neck and went to sleep with the knife in her other hand, and she was soon snoring. But Gerda would not close her eyes; she did not know whether she was to live or to die. The robbers sat round the fire, eating and drinking, and the old woman was turning somersaults. This sight terrified the poor little girl. Then the wood pigeons said, "Coo, coo, we have seen little Kay. His sledge was drawn by a white chicken and he was sitting in the Snow Queen's sledge; it was floating low down over the trees, while we were in our nest. She blew upon us young ones, and they all died except we two; coo, coo."

"What are you saying up there?" asked Gerda. "Where was the Snow Queen going? Do you know anything about it?"

"She was most likely going to Lapland, because there is always snow and ice there! Ask the reindeer who is tied up there."

"There is ice and snow, and it's a splendid place," said the reindeer. "You can run and jump about where you like on those big glittering plains. The Snow Queen has her summer tent there, but her permanent castle is up at the North Pole, on the island which is called Spitzbergen!"

"Oh, Kay, little Kay!" sighed Gerda.

"Lie still, or I shall stick the knife into you!" said the robber girl.

In the morning Gerda told her all that the wood pigeons had said, and the little robber girl looked quite solemn, but she nodded her head and said, "No matter, no matter! Do you know where Lapland is?" she asked the reindeer.

"Who should know better than I," said the animal, its eyes dancing. "I was born and brought up there, and I used to leap about on the snow-fields."

"Listen," said the robber girl. "You see that all our men folks are away, but mother is still here, and she will stay, but later on in the morning she will take a drink out of the big bottle there, and after that she will have a nap—then I will do something for you." Then she jumped out of bed, ran along to her mother and pulled her beard, and said, "Good-morning, my own dear nanny-goat!" And her mother filliped her nose till it was red and blue; but it was all affection.

As soon as her mother had had her draught from the bottle and had dropped asleep, the little robber girl went along to the reindeer, and said, "I should have the greatest pleasure in the world in keeping you here, to tickle you with my knife, because you are such fun then, however, it does not matter. I will untie your halter and help you out-side so that you may run away to Lapland, but you must put your best foot foremost, and take this little girl for me to the Snow Queen's palace, where her playfellow is. I have no doubt you heard what she was telling me, for she spoke loud enough, and you are generally eavesdrop-ping!"

The reindeer jumped into the air for joy. The robber girl lifted little Gerda up, and had the forethought to tie her on, nay, even to give her a little cushion to sit upon. "Here, after all, I will give you your fur boots back, for it will be very cold, but I will keep your muff, it is too pretty to part with. Still you sha'n't be cold. Here are my mother's big mittens for you, they will reach up to your elbows; here, stick your hands in! Now your hands look just like my nasty mother's!"

Gerda shed tears of joy.

"I don't like you to whimper!" said the little robber girl. "You ought to be looking delighted! And here are two loaves and a ham for you, so that you sha'n't starve."

These things were tied on to the back of the reindeer. The little robber girl opened the door, called in all the big dogs, and then she cut the halter with her knife, and said to the reindeer, "Now run, but take care of my little girl!"

Gerda stretched out her hands in the big mittens to the robber girl and said good-by, and then the reindeer darted off over briars and bushes, through the big wood, over swamps and plains, as fast as it could go. The wolves howled and the ravens screamed, while the red lights quivered up in the sky.

"There are my old northern lights," said the reindeer. "See how they flash!" and on it rushed faster than ever, day and night. The loaves were eaten, and the ham, too, and then they were in Lapland.

SIXTH STORY

THE LAPP WOMAN AND THE FINN WOMAN

They stopped by a little hut, a very poverty-stricken one; the roof sloped right down to the ground, and the door was so low that the people had to creep on hands and knees when they wanted to go in or out. There was nobody at home here but an old Lapp woman, who was frying fish over a train-oil lamp. The reindeer told her all Gerda's story, but it told its own first; for it thought it was much the most important. Gerda was so overcome by the cold that she could not speak at all.

"Oh, you poor creature!" said the Lapp woman; "you've got a long way to go yet; you will have to go hundreds of miles into Finmark, for the Snow Queen is paying a country visit there, and she burns blue lights, every night. I will write a few words on a dried stock-fish, for I have no paper. I will give it to you to take to the Finn woman up there. She will be better able to direct you than I can."

So when Gerda was warmed, and had eaten and drunk something, the Lapp woman wrote a few words on a dried stock-fish and gave it to her, bidding her take good care of it. Then she tied her on the reindeer again, and off they flew. Flicker, flicker, went the beautiful blue northern lights up in the sky all night long;—and last they came to Finmark, and knocked on the Finn woman's chimney, for she had no door at all.

There was such a heat inside that the Finn woman went almost naked; she was little and very grubby. She at once loosened Gerda's things, and took off the mittens and the boots, or she would have been too hot. Then she put a piece of ice on the reindeer's head, and after that she read what was written on the stock-fish. She read it three times, and then she knew it by heart, and put the fish into the pot for dinner; there was no reason why it should not be eaten, and she never wasted anything.

Again the reindeer told his own story first, and then little Gerda's. The Finn woman blinked with her wise eyes, but she said nothing.

"You are so clever," said the reindeer. "I know you can bind all the winds of the world with a bit of sewing cotton. When a skipper unties one knot, he gets a good wind, when he unties two, it blows hard, and if he undoes the third and the fourth he brings a storm about his head wild enough to blow down the forest trees. Won't you give the little girl a drink, so that she may have the strength of twelve men to overcome the Snow Queen?"

"The strength of twelve men," said the Finn woman. "Yes, that will be about enough."

She went along to a shelf and took down a big folded skin, which she unrolled. There were curious characters written on it, and the Finn woman read till the perspiration poured down her forehead.

But the reindeer again implored her to give Gerda something, and Gerda looked at her with such beseeching eyes, full of tears, that the Finn woman began blinking again, and drew the reindeer along into a corner, where she whispered to it, at the same time putting fresh ice on its head.

"Little Kay is certainly with the Snow Queen, and he is delighted with everything there. He thinks it is the best place in the world, but that is because he has got a splinter of glass in his heart and a grain of glass in his eye. They will have to come out first, or he will never be human again, and the Snow Queen will keep him in her power!"

"But can't you give little Gerda something to take which will give her power to conquer it all?"

"I can't give her greater power than she already has. Don't you see how great it is? Don't you see how both man and beast have to serve her? How she has got on as well as she has on her bare feet? We must not tell her what power she has; it is in her heart, because she is such a sweet, innocent child. If she can't reach the Snow Queen herself, then we can't help her. The Snow Queen's gardens begin just two miles from here. You can carry the little girl as far as that. Put her down by the big bush standing there in the snow covered with red berries. Don't stand gossiping, but hurry back to me!" Then the Finn woman lifted Gerda on to the reindeer's back, and it rushed off as fast as it could.

"Oh, I have not got my boots, and I have not got my mittens!" cried little Gerda.

She soon felt the want of them in that cutting wind, but the reindeer did not dare to stop. It ran on till it came to the bush with the red berries. There it put Gerda down, and kissed her on the mouth, while big shining tears trickled down its face. Then it ran back again as fast as ever it could. There stood poor little Gerda, without shoes or gloves, in the middle of freezing icebound Finmark.

She ran forward as quickly as she could. A whole regiment of snowflakes came towards her; they did not fall from the sky, for it was quite clear, with the northern lights shining brightly. No; these snowflakes ran along the ground, and the nearer they came the bigger they grew. Gerda remembered well how big and ingenious they looked under the magnifying glass. But the size of these was monstrous, they were alive; they were the Snow Queen's advanced guard, and they took the most curious shapes. Some looked like big, horrid porcupines, some like bundles of knotted snakes with their heads sticking out. Others, again, were like fat little bears with bristling hair, but all were dazzling white, living snowflakes.

Then little Gerda said the Lord's Prayer, and the cold

was so great that her breath froze as it came out of her
mouth, and she could see it like a cloud of smoke in front
of her. It grew thicker and thicker, till it formed itself into
bright little angels who grew bigger and bigger, when they
touched the ground. They all wore helmets and carried
shields and spears in their hands. More and more of them
appeared, and when Gerda had finished her prayer she
was surrounded by a whole legion. They pierced the
snowflakes with their spears and shivered them into a
hundred pieces, and little Gerda walked fearlessly and un-
dauntedly through them. The angels touched her hands
and her feet, and then she hardly felt how cold it was, but
walked quickly on towards the Palace of the Snow Queen.

Now we must see what Kay was about. He was not
thinking about Gerda at all, least of all that she was just
outside the Palace.

SEVENTH STORY

What Happened in the Snow Queen's Palace and Afterwards

The Palace walls were made of drifted snow, and the windows and doors of the biting winds. There were over a
hundred rooms in it, shaped just as the snow had drifted.
The biggest one stretched for many miles. They were all
lighted by the strongest northern lights. All the rooms
were immensely big and empty, and glittering in their ici-
ness. There was never any gaiety in them; not even so
much as a ball for the little bears, when the storms might
have turned up as the orchestra, and the polar bears
might have walked about on their hind legs and shown off
their grand manners. There was never even a little game-
playing party, for such games as "touch last" or "the biter
bit"—no, not even a little gossip over the coffee cups for
the white fox-girls. Immense, vast, and cold were the
Snow Queen's halls. The northern lights came and went
with such regularity that you could count the seconds between their coming and going. In the midst of these never-
ending snow-halls was a frozen lake. It was broken up on

the surface into a thousand bits, but each was so exactly like the others that the whole formed a perfect work of art. The Snow Queen sat in the very middle of it when she sat at home. She then said that she was sitting on "The Mirror of Reason," and that it was the best and only one in the world.

Little Kay was blue with cold, nay, almost black; but he did not know it, for the Snow Queen had kissed away the icy shiverings, and his heart was little better than a lump of ice. He went about dragging some sharp, flat pieces of ice, which he placed in all sorts of patterns, trying to make something out of them; just like the little tablets of wood, with which we make patterns, and call them a "Chinese puzzle."

Kay's patterns were most ingenious, because they were the "Ice puzzles of Reason." In his eyes they were first-rate and of the greatest importance. This was because of the grain of glass still in his eye. He made many patterns forming words, but he could never find out the right way to place them for one particular word, a word he was most anxious to make. It was "Eternity." The Snow Queen had said to him that if he could find out this word he should be his own master, and she would give him the whole world and a new pair of skates. But he could not discover it.

"Now I am going to fly away to the warm countries," said the Snow Queen. "I want to go and peep into the black cauldrons!" She meant the volcanoes Etna and Vesuvius by this. "I must whiten them a little; it does them good, and the lemons and the grapes, too!" And away she flew.

Kay sat quite alone in all those many miles of empty ice halls. He looked at his bits of ice, and thought and thought, till something gave way within him. He sat so stiff and immovable that one might have thought he was frozen to death.

Then it was that little Gerda walked into the Palace, through the great gates in a biting wind. She said her evening prayer, and the wind dropped as if lulled to sleep, and she walked on into the big empty hall. She saw Kay, and knew him at once. She flung her arms round his neck, held him fast, and cried, "Kay, little Kay, have I found you at last?"

But he sat still, rigid and cold.

Then little Gerda shed hot tears; they fell upon his breast and penetrated to his heart. Here they thawed the lump of ice, and melted the little bit of the mirror which was in it. He looked at her, and she sang:

> "Where roses deck the flowery vale,
> There, Infant Jesus, we Thee hail!"

Then Kay burst into tears. He cried so much that the grain of glass was washed out of his eye. He knew her, and shouted with joy, "Gerda, dear little Gerda! Where have you been for such a long time? And where have I been?"

He looked round and said, "How cold it is here; how empty and vast!" He kept tight hold of Gerda, who laughed and cried for joy. Their happiness was so heavenly that even the bits of ice danced for joy around them; and when they settled down, there they lay! just in the very position the Snow Queen had told Kay he must find out, if he was to become his own master and have the whole world and a new pair of skates.

Gerda kissed his cheeks and they grew rosy, she kissed his eyes and they shone like hers, she kissed his hands and his feet, and he became well and strong. The Snow Queen might come home whenever she liked. His order of release was written there in shining letters of ice.

They took hold of each other's hands and wandered out of the big Palace. They talked about grandmother, and about the roses upon the roof. Wherever they went, the wind lay still and the sun broke through the clouds. When they reached the bush with the red berries, they found the reindeer waiting for them, and he had brought another young reindeer with him, whose udders were full. The children drank her warm milk and kissed her on the mouth. Then they carried Kay and Gerda, first to the Finn woman, in whose heated hut they warmed themselves and received directions about the homeward journey. Then they went on to the Lapp woman. She had made new clothes for them and prepared her sledge. Both the reindeer ran by their side, to the boundaries of the country. Here the first green buds appeared, and they said "Goodby" to the reindeer and the Lapp woman. They heard the first little birds twittering and saw the buds in the forest. Out of it came riding a young girl on a beautiful horse, which Gerda knew, for it had drawn the golden chariot. She had a scarlet cap on her head and pistols in her belt; it was the little robber girl, who was tired of being at home. She was riding northward to see how she liked it before she tried some other part of the world. She knew them again, and Gerda recognized her with delight.

"You are a nice fellow to go tramping off!" she said to little Kay. "I should like to know if you deserve to have somebody running to the end of the world for your sake!"

But Gerda patted her cheek and asked about the Prince and Princess.

"They are traveling in foreign countries," said the robber girl.

"But the crow?" asked Gerda.

"Oh, the crow is dead!" she answered. "The tame sweetheart is a widow, and goes about with a bit of black wool tied round her leg. She pities herself bitterly, but it's all nonsense! But tell me how you got on, yourself, and where you found him."

Gerda and Kay both told her all about it.

"Snip, snap, snurre, it's all right at last then!" she said, and she took hold of their hands and promised that, if she ever passed through their town, she would pay them a visit. Then she rode off into the wide world. But Kay and Gerda walked on, hand in hand, and wherever they went, they found the most delightful spring and blooming flowers. Soon they recognized the big town where they lived, with its tall towers, in which the bells still rang their merry peals. They went straight on to the grandmother's door, up the stairs and into her room. Everything was just as they had left it, and the old clock ticked in the corner, and the hands pointed to the time. As they went through the door into the room they perceived that they were grown up. The roses clustered round the open window, and there stood their two little chairs. Kay and Gerda sat down upon them, still holding each other by the hand. All the cold empty grandeur of the Snow Queen's palace had passed from their memory like a bad dream. Grandmother sat in God's warm sunshine reading from her Bible.

"Without ye become as little children ye cannot enter into the Kingdom of Heaven."

Kay and Gerda looked into each other's eyes and then all at once the meaning of the old hymn came to them.

> "Where roses deck the flowery vale,
> There, Infant Jesus, we Thee hail!"

And there they both sat, grown up and yet children, children at heart; and it was summer—warm, beautiful summer.